Praise for the June Jenson Series

"Emily Harper has a very distinctive writing style and all of her books have something in common – they contain a lot of laugh-out-loud moments, feisty, opinionated and loveable heroines and a fast-paced action filled storyline."
–*Cosmochicklitan*

"This is a hugely action-packed book and it's all kinds of ridiculous, in the best sense… my favourite of her novels so far." –*Reviewed the Book*

"June Jenson and the Shield of Quell is a fun story that will have you hooked from page one, with some very lovable quirky main characters and lots of intrigue." –*Alba in Bookland*

"I found this to be a gripping mystery novel. It had some wonderful gentle humour sprinkled through it… Harper has given life to a wonderful array of characters. Each one helps move the story along and keeps us entertained with their antics." –*Whispering Stories*

JUNE JENSON
AND THE
KING'S LOST
TREASURE
(BOOK THREE)

EMILY HARPER

ISBN-13 9780994896469

For my Aunty Lynda May. Words cannot express my gratitude for everything you have done, and continue to do for me, but I thought I would try anyways. You are a rare and beautiful woman who makes the world a better place just by being in it.

Thank you.

ACKNOWLEDGMENTS

To my wonderful editor, Emily Ferko, who has been apart of this wonderful adventure since the beginning—thank you my friend. To my friends and family who support me in all of my crazy endeavours—I love you, and I thank you. And finally to the readers who have been with June from the beginning, I hope I've made you proud.

Chapter One

"Did you get it?" Simon Locke asks.

"Simon, I've only just come through the door." I speak into the phone held up to my ear and balance my bag, keys and the courier package precariously. "You'll have to give me a moment."

"This is top priority, June," Simon says in that upbeat, condescending tone I've come to know all too well. "Deadlines, I'm afraid. The network wants to make this their big fall production and we have to hit the ground running before someone scoops it. This is a hot commodity; I would think you would be frothing at the mouth for this."

I roll my eyes. *Everything* is a priority with the network. But that's the thing with show business that I've come to learn: it's so fast paced that things really do need to be a priority. Tomorrow it will be irrelevant.

But Simon does have a tendency to exaggerate, I reason. And lie. Like the time he had his employee, Clint, pose as the Professor and Dr Cooke's intern in order to film them and write a full exposé of our excavation in Colorado.

Now Clint seems like a part of the family. Well, a very reluctant member, but every family has to have one of those. Travelling around the world with the Professor, Dr Cooke, Griffin and myself to film the segments for *Blast from the Past*, Britain's new archaeology show, has forced Clint to become part of the fold.

"Alright, I'm opening the package now," I say, placing my bag on the foyer table and ripping open the top of the courier package. I peer inside, but there is only a single piece of paper. "You haven't given me much to go on, I see."

"I don't have much," Simon says. I can imagine him tapping his fingers on his desk, and willing me to hurry up. "The less information that is out there the better, I say. Every news station would be all over this otherwise."

I scan the paper and commit it to memory. Even if I didn't have an eidetic memory it wouldn't be hard, as there really isn't much on it.

"So, this man has just called you up, out of the blue, and wants to sell his ring?" I ask, raising my eyebrows.

"Well, he didn't call me, he called a friend of mine," Simon explains, and his lack of further explanation makes me certain this friend might not be on the up and up.

"And he thinks it is King Solomon's ring? As in the biblical king who was able to control demons with said ring?" I don't try to hide my scepticism. "Who is this man? How would he have any idea what the ring is or who it

2

belonged to? You've just given me his address with the flimsiest description of what it looks like. It's not much to go on, is it?"

"Quite frankly, I don't want to ask him any more until we are able to get there," Simon explains. "I don't want him to fully grasp what he might have."

"Hmm… that's not very ethical," I say.

"June, he's requested ten thousand pounds in small bills. I'm not entirely sure ethics are really going to be a part of the equation here."

I frown, knowing *exactly* how I feel about that.

My head whips up at the sound of raised voices coming from upstairs.

"Listen, Simon, ethics aside, this is not a very good time," I say as the voices upstairs get louder. "The Professor is at a very tricky stage with his new medication, and I'm not sure I should uproot him right now for a wild goose chase."

"June, I understand… really, I do," he says, though his tone says otherwise. "But this isn't going to wait."

"What if I go on my own and scout it out?" I suggest.

"Not going to work, June," Simon sighs. "The viewers want to see you and the Professor *together*! We need the whole team on this one."

This makes me soften, though only slightly. Even while I was teaching at Oxford University, before I was let go for… *creative differences*, my knowledge and expertise was hardly ever sought after. Quite frankly, I got the feeling most days that my students were just there to get attendance credit. But the viewership from the show has been overwhelming. People stop us in the street to tell us how much they enjoy the program. We've even been asked for pictures and autographs.

Well, the Professor has. But, they used my pen.

"The ratings are still strong then?" I ask.

"Solid June, very solid. People can't get enough of the Professor and his faithful sidekick."

"Faithful sidekick?" I repeat, standing up straighter. I'm supposed to be the main host of the show, not the bloody sidekick.

"Yes, Dr Cooke," Simon chuckles. "What a pair they are."

I sniff and push my black rimmed glasses further up my nose.

"Modern day Laurel and Hardy is what people are calling them," Simon says. "The video of the two of them getting chased by the ostriches in Africa... I nearly wet myself watching it."

"Well, I would hope people would be watching for the history," I say tightly.

"Oh, they like that too, I'm sure," Simon says. "Anyways, I have you all scheduled for a flight Friday morning. Clint will meet you at the airport."

"Listen Simon," I say, but he interrupts.

"June, I know about the Professor, and I appreciate your predicament. But you signed on for a six episode contract to be scheduled at our discretion, and we want the both of you. You're a package deal. This is the last one before we can enter into contract renegotiations, and we need to get this done. This is the lost treasure of King Solomon we are talking about. Forget Sutton-Hoo, Cassidy's Coins—they are pittance to this discovery!"

A familiar feeling of restlessness stirs in my chest. I want to do this. If it were just me, I would already be on the plane.

But it's not just me. It hasn't been just me for a very long time.

"I'll let you know this evening," I say, and before he can respond I end the call.

Keeping the paper in my hand, I make my way up the staircase towards the Professor's bedroom. I creep up to the half open door, trying not to make a sound as I peer through the opening at the Professor's agitated face.

"I said I'm not eating that!" The Professor yells and practically throws the bowl back at Mrs Stevens. "You've put something in it."

"I bloody have not!" she yells back. "The cheek! It's the same old shite that you eat every day, nothing added, I can assure you!"

She slams the bowl down on the table next to the Professor's bed and scowls at him.

"Well, I'm not eating it!" he says, turning his nose up at the dish.

"You'll bloody well eat it, even if I have to ram it down your throat one spoon full at a time!" she bellows back at him.

I raise my eyebrows at her tone, but then straighten and remember I hired this woman for a reason. She's the only person I have ever seen the Professor cower under, and if my years of taking care of the Professor have taught me anything it's that a soft touch is ineffective. He never listened to me: not about medication, about alcohol, about driving. And he must follow the doctor's precise instructions in order for this new trial medication to work and stop his mind from deteriorating further.

A firm hand is what he needs. It's the only hope we have.

"I saw you ground those pills up and put them in the porridge when I wasn't looking," he accuses, pointing his finger at Mrs Stevens.

"If you weren't looking, how could you see a bleedin' thing?" she asks, crossing her large arms over her ample bosom. Her hair is pulled away from her face with a tattered scarf and the red splotches on her cheeks pronounce the fact she isn't wearing a stitch of makeup. I've been told she doesn't have time for that sort of nonsense. Not that I asked. She barked the information at me when I asked her if she had seen my mascara.

"I could hear you grinding them," he mutters, pulling his covers up to his neck, his blue eyes magnified behind his metal-rimmed spectacles. "It was either the pills or your massive teeth."

"I'm going to go and make a cup of tea for us," she says in low voice, which causes the Professor to pull the blankets tighter to his chest. "And when I get back, there better not be a speck of food left in that bowl."

With that she spins on her heels and storms away from the bed. Even though I can see her coming I jump a little as she whips the door open.

"He's absolutely impossible!" she yells, before stomping passed me.

I let out the breath I wasn't aware I was holding and slowly make my way in the room. I stop just through the door and shake my head.

The Professor is propped up in bed by his pillows, glaring at the retreating back of Mrs Stevens. At the foot of the bed is Dr Cooke, also propped up by pillows. Dr Cooke joyfully spoons his own porridge into his mouth.

"Who are we, the Buckets?" I ask, my eyes shifting between Dr Cooke and the Professor. "Who should I be calling Grandpa Joe?"

"Who?" The Professor frowns.

"The family from Charlie and the Chocolate Factory have a similar set up," I gesture to the two of them.

"Do they?" the Professor asks, raising his eyebrows.

"Have I met them?"

A ghost of a smile appears on my face as my heart dips a little in my chest.

"It was my favourite book as a child. You used to read it to me almost every night, remember?" I prompt. "Charlie goes to a chocolate factory when he finds the golden ticket?"

"I wouldn't mind some chocolate," the Professor muses, sitting up a little straighter and turning his attention to Dr Cooke. "Daniel?"

"Maybe some chocolate biscuits with the tea?" Dr Cooke suggests.

"You know, when I agreed to Dr Cooke coming to live with us, I wasn't aware this was going to be the arrangement," I say, raising my eyebrows.

"Oh, Daniel sleeps next door in the evenings," the Professor waves away the concern. "It's just more prudent for us to be resting in the same room during the day so Mrs Stevens doesn't have to make so many trips."

"She's not meant to be your servant!" I say, shaking my head. "She's here to give you your medicine and check up on you."

"We expanded her job description," the Professor explains. "She was too idle, and kept fussing over me with that bloody arm cuff contraption."

"That's exactly what I hired her to do," I remind him, placing my hands on my hips. "Not to make your tea and porridge."

"Which reminds me!" He peers past me to see if Mrs Stevens is out of sight and picks up the bowl of porridge he previously refused. He starts to spoon it in his mouth.

"I thought you weren't going to eat that?" I try to hide my smile.

"She loves it when I put up a fight," the Professor winks, his white hair sticking up on one side. "She fancies me."

"Mrs Stevens?" I ask, and quickly whip my head towards the door thinking she must be standing there and this is another wind up.

"Can't get enough of me. Hovers over me all day, doesn't she, Daniel?" the Professor asks, and puts another spoonful in his mouth.

"Love sick! Never leaves him alone," Dr Cooke nods, still eating his own porridge.

"Hmm, that's her job though, isn't it?" I ask, and tuck my short brown hair behind my ear.

"Beyond the call of duty, June. She's got it bad," the Professor says and places his half empty bowl back down on the table before picking up his comb. I watch as he runs it through his hair only making more of a mess of it.

"And do you—er—I mean…" I look towards the door and frown.

"You know, your grandmother wasn't a particularly attractive woman," the Professor says, taking off his glasses and using the edge of the duvet to wipe them. "I would have described her as hearty."

"You've always said I was the spitting image of her," I say, trying not to sound insulted.

The Professor ignores my comment and put his glasses back on.

"And Mrs Stevens... Well, that woman has the thickest ankles I've ever seen," the Professor says wistfully.

Right then.

"How are you both feeling today?" I ask as the Professor reaches for his journal and begins to write in it.

"Right as rain," he says, his eyes not leaving the paper as the pen begins to scrawl. "Though Daniel had a bit of a spell earlier."

The Professor has always kept journals, ever since he was a student at Oxford. The pages used to be filled with his daily activities, notes about historical pieces or sites he was working on.

Then his early diagnosis of Alzheimer's combined with the accusation that he stole an artefact from one of his excavation digs at Sutton-Hoo sent him into a downward spiral. His journal writing became his obsession, as he jotted down hundreds of conspiracy theories. It was only when he was exonerated from the crime that his writing returned to more simple topics.

"Are you alright?" I turn to Dr Cooke in concern.

"Yes, quite alright, thank you dear," Dr Cooke nods,

but narrows his eyes at the Professor's derisive snort.

"He fainted as I was having my blood work done," the Professor explains, pointing to his journal. "Got the entire episode all down here."

"I had a diabetic attack. It was nothing to do with your blood," Dr Cooke scoffs. "I want you to change that journal entry immediately!"

The Professor pretends not to hear him.

"But you're all right now, are you?" I ask him.

"I could do with a bit more blanket," Dr Cooke says, tugging at his end and glaring at the Professor when the blanket doesn't budge.

"Is your lad back yet?" The Professor ignores him.

"Griffin's home tomorrow," I answer.

"You should have gone with him," the Professor says. "A little sun and relaxation would have done you good."

"Visiting Griffin's Mum and her new husband in Tenerife would not have been relaxing, I can assure you," I say, shaking my head.

"I'll never understand how that woman somehow convinced two men to marry her, and yet you're still unattached," the Professor says in an idle tone as he turns the page of the journal.

"Oh, thank you very much!" I say, frowning. "And I'm not *unattached*. Griffin and I live together."

"Yes, but he hasn't chiselled anything in stone, has he?" the Professor asks.

"He's testing the jam, without buying the jar," Dr Cooke agrees.

I look at the two of them and for a moment I'm speechless.

"Chiselled what? We aren't in the stone age!" I say. "Besides, maybe I don't want to get married…"

Mrs Stevens returns with the tray of tea and biscuits and looks at the half empty porridge bowl beside the Professor but makes no comment.

"Keep this up any longer and you'll end up a spinster, June," the Professor says and flicks his eyes in the direction of Mrs Stevens. "Such a waste."

Unsure now as to whether he is referring to me or the well-endowed Mrs Stevens, I purse my lips.

"Not that I am a spinster, but there is nothing wrong with not getting married," I argue. I ignore the slight twinge in my chest as I say this. "It's a new day and age… And besides, I would hardly have time while looking after you two. Apparently you're too ill to even get up!"

I'm not even sure marriage is something that's important to me. I've always had greater focuses in my life. Like the Professor, and my career.

And yes, now that the Professor is getting older and he has Dr Cooke and Mrs Stevens I'm not needed as much, but that doesn't mean I'm not needed at all.

And yes, my career has taken a drastic turn in the last year, which gives me much more time to myself. But I fill that time with important things. Like reading, and writing, and… er… gardening.

Well I just trimmed the hedge in the front yard, but it's something, isn't it?

"Maybe you are sending your young lad the wrong signals," Mrs Stevens suggests as she hands the Professor and Dr Cooke their cups of tea, before handing me the last cup on the tray.

"What 'signal' is that?" I ask her before I can stop myself. Honestly, this is absolutely ridiculous. I'm not sure how we even got onto this topic. I don't want to get married. Well, I don't *need* to get married.

"Well, is that how you've always done your hair?" she asks me.

"Er—yes…" I say, bringing my hand to my chin length, wavy brown hair.

What's wrong with my hair?

"Oh, alright. It can't be that, then. I didn't know if you made a bit more of an effort with it when you were first together."

"More of an…" I bluster. "What is *that* supposed to mean?"

"Maybe it's the glasses," Dr Cooke chimes in.

"What's wrong with my glasses?" I ask, and instinctively push them further up my nose.

"Oh, they're fine," Dr Cooke replies quickly. "I only meant they draw attention to the fact you don't really do much to your face. I've always thought you looked lovely with a little rouge."

I open my mouth to retort, but the Professor speaks before I get a chance.

"June's face is fine," he says, patting my hand and I soften. "It's those clothes and that god-awful bag she's always carting around that are the real issue."

"I—" I straighten my back and remove my hand from his. "I love that bloody bag and you know it!"

I look down at my clothes, and honestly, they're not *that* bad. A nice clean pair of trousers and a button down blouse, tucked in. Practical and classic, I assure myself. I've never been one for patterns or prints. For the majority of my adult life I lived under a cloud of suspicion when the Professor was accused of stealing the priceless relic from Sutton-Hoo. I did everything possible to avoid any attention, and that included modest dress. And since he was acquitted of the scandal a few years ago—well, old habits die hard, I'm afraid.

Also, these trousers happen to be very comfortable.

And my bag. My brown leather knapsack has seen me through so much, it has been everywhere with me.

I'm quite attached to that bag.

"As I've always said, June Bug, never ask questions you don't want the answers to," the Professor tells me.

"I never asked!" I argue, and take a deep breath, attempting to calm myself down. "Besides, I happen to have a very fulfilling life, and I don't need to get married."

"See, now there's the spirit," Mrs Stevens collects the tray with the dirty dishes before making her way to the bedroom door. "Then you won't be disappointed when no one asks."

I choke on some of my tea and it dribbles down my chin.

"God I love to watch that woman waddle," the Professor says, peering past me to the now empty doorway.

"Listen, as much as I love hearing about my doomed marital status, I did come in here for a purpose," I say, resting my cup of tea on my knee.

"Oh?" the Professor says, reaching for his journal once again.

"Have the new jam jars arrived?" Dr Cooke asks, his eyes lighting up.

"Er—I'm not sure," I say, shaking my head. "I've had a call from Simon."

"Oh," Dr Cooke sighs, deflated, while the Professor continues to read something he just wrote in his journal.

The two of them used to be so eager for a glimpse of adventure and now they barely want to leave their bed.

"Yes, well, he's sent this," I say, handing the paper in my hand to Dr Cooke. "It seems a very interesting project."

Dr Cooke scans the page and snorts.

"The lost treasure of King Solomon?" He shakes his

head and hands the paper to the Professor. "It hasn't been seen or heard of in centuries."

I turn to look at the Professor as he studies the sheet.

"Well?" I prompt.

"They have nothing," he says, putting the paper down beside him and reaching again for his journal. "They've found someone who is attempting to sell a gold ring on the black market. It could be anything. It could be nothing. Probably out to make a quick few."

My shoulders sink at his words.

"But… But you don't *know* that it is nothing!" I argue.

"That paper says that the description of the ring *could* potentially be something related to King Solomon because of the markings—it could be *anything*. A copy, another ring from the same era, a forgery…" he argues right back.

"Yes, but… it could *not* be. Don't you—don't you want to *know?*" I look at the two of them perplexed. It's like I am not looking at the same two men who my whole life have carted me off on a thousand wild goose chases, in the hopes that maybe, just once it wouldn't be.

The Professor just shrugs.

"I—I can't believe this!" I yell at them both. "This is the lost treasure of King Solomon I am talking about and the two of you are sitting there like you can't be bothered."

Dr Cooke sighs. "June, archaeology is a young man's game—"

"No, it's not!" I interrupt. "It's a dying art, for exactly

the opposite reason."

"It's a lot to constantly get on a plane," Dr Cooke sulks. "Can't they just send the picture of the ring here? Why do we need to go all the way to Cairo?"

"I don't believe what I'm hearing…" I shake my head. "I can't believe I am standing here, trying to convince you two to come on an adventure with me."

"You're always telling me I'm too unwell to do things; I'm finally agreeing with you," the Professor points out.

"Yes, but that's what we *do*, isn't it?" I ask, throwing my arms up in the air. "You say you want to come. I say you can't because its too dangerous, and then you weasel your way into coming somehow anyways!"

"Weasel?" the Professor sits up straighter. "Listening to you someone may think we somehow intrude on your life."

Both look affronted.

"You do!" I say to them. "But that's half the fun, isn't it?"

"Well, we won't *intrude* this time, will we, Daniel?" the Professor says.

"Certainly not," Dr Cooke agrees tersely.

"That's not what I meant and you know it. I just can't believe the two of you want this," I gesture at the bed and the teacups, "to be the rest of your lives."

"I'm tired," the Professor says, crossing his arms across his chest. "She's taken away my bloody whiskey and put me on a gluttonous diet!"

"It's a gluten-free diet," I correct him.

"She's taken away my jam," he sulks.

"If you come with me, you can have jam and scones for breakfast every day," I coax.

He studies me for a minute before sighing.

"What's the point?" he asks. "She'll only take them away when I get back."

"This doesn't sound like you," I frown. "You're usually the first one out of the door when something exciting comes along."

"My knees hurt," he waves his hand to the end of the bed.

"I'll get you braces," I say.

"And they don't make my tea right in foreign countries," he argues.

"So, what?" I ask, shaking my head. "You're just giving up?"

"It's called retirement," the Professor says. "And we find it suits us well."

Retirement? I'm not sure that's a word I have ever heard out of his mouth before.

"And you agree with him?" I ask Dr Cooke.

"Well…" he starts.

"Daniel is retiring too. We are going to rest now and make jam," the Professor interrupts. "Well, I'll make it and he'll eat it. Unless she bloody takes it off him as well."

"What's all the shouting about?" Mrs Stevens says from behind me, and I jump at her voice.

"I—," I hesitate at her intimidating stare but continue. "I was trying to convince these two to come to Egypt with me to have a look at a ring."

"Never buy your own engagement ring, dear," Mrs Stevens pats my shoulder. "It sends a very *needy* message. He'll ask you one day, I'm sure."

"Not a ring for me," I say through gritted teeth. "It's potentially an important historical relic, and I want these two to come with me to validate the piece."

"Oh," she nods. "Well, in that case, absolutely not. He's in too fragile of a state. I've only just got his blood pressure back under control."

"Of course I would never dream of doing it if I thought it would be detrimental to the Professor's health," I say, feeling the need to defend myself. "I would closely monitor him at all times, and you are welcome to come with us as well if you think it would help."

"I can't fly; I've got a bad hernia." She points to a small bulge in her shirt.

"Oh good God," I say, before I catch myself. "Er— the network will also be providing medical care for the Professor in Cairo should he need it."

"It won't do," she says shaking her head. "I'm afraid the answer is no."

"No?" I say, raising one eyebrow. "I'm sorry, I didn't

know that this was your decision to make."

"He's *my* patient," she says, straightening her back and staring at me.

"And he's *my* grandfather," I say, straightening my own to try and match her intimidating height.

"If anyone is at all concerned, I also don't think I should go," Dr Cooke raises his arm from the bed.

"When's the last time you two left this room?" I ask, looking around at the stacked books and piles of papers.

"Daniel and I had tea in the garden with you yesterday," the Professor waves his hand.

"That was two weeks ago," I argue, looking up at Mrs Stevens, who has her hands on her hips. "He should be getting up and about."

"He needs to stay comfortable." She narrows her eyes at me. "It's the best thing for him."

"Says who?" I ask her.

"He's gone four days without a single episode," she says, lifting her chin in pride.

"Because he hasn't been able to do anything to forget," I argue, turning to look back at the Professor. "You shouldn't stay cooped up like this."

"I'm fine," he says, patting my hand before reaching for his pen again. "Besides Karen has just taken Mitch back on Eastenders."

"This is ridiculous," I say to him. "Yes, you have to take your medication and scale back a bit, but you still have to live your life."

"You know, I am a certified healthcare practitioner," Mrs Stevens says, and swoops in front of me to check the Professor's temperature. "I think I know what I am doing."

"He doesn't have a fever, he's fine!" I shake my head.

"I think I will decide that," she says, taking the thermometer out of the Professor's mouth and studying it. "Hmm…"

"I think I'd like mine checked as well," Dr Cooke says, putting the back of his hand to his forehead.

"Oh for God's sake, you're both fine!" I shout at them.

"Don't you want him to be as comfortable as possible?" Mrs Stevens asks me. "I mean, I was under the impression that this was the reason for me being here."

"Of course I do," I say. "But I still want him to be… *him.*"

"I think it is time you face the reality of the situation," Mrs Stevens says to me, shaking the thermometer in my direction. "These men are not young anymore. They need proper care and rest."

"Well, they're certainly not going to sit here in bed and waste away," I say to her, my hands on my hips. "I appreciate everything you are doing for my grandfather, I really do. But he is an archaeologist. He belongs in the field, discovering history, with me."

"You're living in the past, girl," Mrs Stevens shakes her head. "Some days he doesn't even know who he is. Do you want to make that worse by dragging him out on some cockamamie adventure that could turn out to be nothing?"

"But it could turn out to be everything!" I retort, and turn to the Professor. "It's the lost treasure of *King Solomon*. This would be one of the greatest discoveries the world has ever seen! I just cannot allow you to not want to be a part of it."

And suddenly it is very important for him to understand. This isn't about me, or him. This is about history. Some of the most important history this world will ever know, and that's not something I would have ever imagined him to turn down.

"If I didn't think you could do this, I would have already told the network no," I say to him.

The Professor looks from Mrs Stevens glaring face to my beseeching one.

"We can do this," I say to him.

"I don't know, June," the Professor sighs, shaking his head.

I gulp down the panic that rises in my chest. This is my new worry in life, and I realize it is a full turnaround. Before it was whether he was going to take his trousers off in public, or whether he would find the key to the liquor cabinet. But no, it is this complete lack of energy, of will, that now has me absolutely heartbroken. Before I felt a fighting chance, but this acceptance of his circumstance and life is terrifying to me.

And it just won't do.

"One more adventure," I say to him, putting my hand on his knee.

He looks at me earnestly and we study each other.

The lines around his eyes are becoming increasingly deep, magnified by the silver rimmed spectacles that sit on the bridge of his nose. But his bright blue eyes are still lively and I can see a hint of excitement in them, whether he wants to acknowledge it or not. He's still there: my grandfather. The man who has dedicated his life to the discovery and preservation of our world's history.

And I realize that I don't care what it takes, or what I have to do—this is what makes my grandfather the man who he is, and I will protect that with whatever power I have in this world. And until that light extinguishes in his eyes, I'll know I have not have fully lost him.

"One more adventure," the Professor tests the words.

"I want it on record that I thoroughly disputed this decision!" Mrs Stevens sniffs from behind me.

"Noted," I nod, still smiling at the Professor.

"Daniel?" he raises his eyebrow at Dr Cooke.

"Oh, alright," Dr Cooke sighs, pulling the blanket further up his chest. "But I'm not bloody sitting in coach!"

Chapter Two

"I've only just got back," Griffin moans as he sits on the bed, and watches me carefully pack the suitcase with everything we might need. "I had a brilliant idea for a new play on the journey home, and I wanted to get cracking with it."

I hold up my chisel and frown, wondering if I should pack it. It could come in handy, but at the same time it has caused quite a bit of trouble with airport security in the past.

"Griffin, we don't have much of a choice here," I say to him, deciding to pack my full tool kit just in case. "This is very time sensitive. We need to get there and speak to this man before someone else finds out—or he tries to sell it to a different buyer."

"I don't know why you even need me to go," he argues.

"They want all of us there, in case we actually find something so we can begin filming right away," I explain to him. "Please don't give me a hard time; I've just managed to convince the other two to go."

"They only want me to go because I look like a prat on television," Griffin says.

"You do not," I say, rolling my eyes. "You always get the '*Oh, he's so dreamy!*' comments. Where as I always get the '*What's up her arse?*' comments, but you don't hear me complaining."

"That's only from the women. The men think I'm a joke, and you're the stuck-up hottie."

"They do?" I say, my head popping up from over the top of the suitcase. "Someone said I was a hottie?"

I'm not entirely sure why, but I feel my face heat, and I can't help but crack a small smile.

"You've got that mysterious librarian thing going on," Griffin says matter-of-factly. "Men like that."

Well, I never.

"Where as I'm just the poor sod who ends up looking like a git trailing after those two," he says, pointing to the hallway.

"You do not!" I argue.

"When the Professor got lured into one of those naughty massage parlours in Beijing, I was the one who ran after him and fell through the open man hole," Griffin says, shaking his head. "Nearly broke my bloody neck. And people still yell out to me in the street to watch where I'm going while they're bent over having a laugh."

"Wasn't the Great Wall of China brilliant?" I ask. "Who would have thought I would get to teach people about one of the seven wonders on national television?"

"And when we went on that African safari, and Dr

Cooke's hat blew off," Griffin says, "I was the one who had to get out of the bloody car, with wild animals all about, to go and get it. I nearly died."

"They were only wild ostriches," I say, trying to suppress my laughter.

"I was nearly pecked to death!" Griffin says, rubbing his arm that was bandaged for a week after the incident.

"Oh, but remember the Yoruba crowns," I say, and get lost in the memory. "The bead work was incredible. I hadn't really studied African history too closely while I was at Oxford but my God, it is beautiful. The colours…"

"Yeah, bloody breath-taking," Griffin mutters under his breath.

There's a loud bang at the door.

"I've bubble wrapped the humidifier, June Bug," the Professor announces squeezing himself and the box through the doorway.

"*I* packed the bloody thing!" Dr Cooke says, following behind him.

"We can't take that with us." I frown at the box, trying to see his face over it. "How are we going to cart that around with us?"

"Clive can carry it," the Professor suggests.

"Clint," I correct as the Professor can never seem to remember Clint's name. "And he won't be able to, he's the cameraman—how is he meant to carry that around?"

"Well, Andrew the boom technician can then. If he's

not too busy listening to someone's private conversations," he says.

I roll my eyes.

"I don't know why you get so uptight about him recording you. That's his *job*. Besides, he isn't coming. The network is only sending Clint with us in case this turns out to be a bit of a ruse," I explain.

"Well, what are we going for then if they don't even believe in it enough to send Andrew?" Griffin pipes in.

"We will need an interpreter and the hired car only fits six people. They've hired a driver that can also interpret for us and will meet us in Cairo," I say. "And can you stop moaning, I've already had to put up with these two all day."

I reach over and take the box out of the Professor's arms.

"I already agreed on your seven different flavours of preserves and Dr Cooke's entire stamp collection. The humidifier is a no," I say sternly.

"Oh, I guess we won't need our medication either then!" the Professor turns to Dr Cooke. "Trying to breathe through that dry air, we'll end up dead before the week is up anyways."

"What about the silver tea set?" Dr Cooke asks, holding up a small box.

"They have tea sets there," I say in exasperation.

"Oh, I suppose we are to just drink our tea from whatever clay pot they hand us?" the Professor scoffs, and storms out of the room.

Dr Cooke looks down at the box before looking up at me.

"The tea box, perhaps?" he suggests.

"I tell you what, if you can fit that into your carry-on, you're more than welcome."

"The tea box is in!" Dr Cooke yells down the hall ad chases after the Professor.

"How was your Mum?" I ask Griffin and sit down on the white embroidered bedspread to start folding my freshly laundered blouses. "Enjoying married life?"

"I suppose," Griffin shrugs and crosses his arms. "I'm still not sure about Rupert. I mean, why did he have to move her all the way to Tenerife?"

Honestly, Griffin is hopeless when it comes to his mother, which usually drives me up the wall. Almost as much as *she* drives me up the wall. But now that she is over two thousand miles away I find it much easier just to smile and nod.

"I bet her knees don't mind that lovely Spanish air," I say.

"Hmm," he nods, but doesn't look convinced. "You know, the area where their house is looked a bit shifty."

"She lives in a retirement community," I remind him and try my best to stop my eyes midroll. "No one in a five mile radius of her house still have their own teeth."

"Exactly! They're all easy prey for some shyster to

come along and take advantage of them," he argues.

"Some shyster?" I raise my eyebrows. "I couldn't see some shyster getting one over on your mother. She'd probably have him giving *her* money by the end of it just to get out of there."

"Hmm, maybe." Griffin nods, and I can tell he isn't really listening.

I casually run my hands over my grey trousers before checking the buttons on my cardigan are still done up.

"Griffin," I hedge as I add the now folded blouses into the suitcase. "Do you like the way that I dress?"

He looks up at me and frowns. "You look fine, why?"

Hmm... I'm not sure *fine* is what I was looking for.

"What about my hair?" I say, tucking the inevitable loose curl behind my ear. "I was thinking of maybe making a change."

"Why? It looks fine the way it is," he says.

There's that word again: *fine.*

"Well is there anything about me that isn't *fine?*" I ask.

"Er—I feel like there is a right answer, and I'm not going to say it," Griffin says, tentatively.

I narrow my eyes at him but choose not to respond.

"June, it's no good. I can't go," the Professor comes back into the room shaking his head.

"What now?" I sigh.

"The bloody television recorder is broken," he says, holding up the recorder, now in two pieces with broken cords dangling from it.

"What happened to it?" I ask.

"He said it was giving him cheek because there was no room left on it for more of his Eastenders," Dr Cooke pops up from behind the Professor and pushes his way into the room.

"Well, if you hadn't recorded all of those rubbish Changing Rooms reruns there would have been more room on the bloody thing, wouldn't there?" the Professor argues while Dr Cooke gasps in outrage.

"How dare you! Rubbish show... Carol Smillie is a *national treasure!*" Dr Cooke retorts.

"Would you two stop it," I yell, standing up and taking the recorder out of the Professor's hands. "Griffin will fix it. You two can stop having a go at each other."

"I don't know how to fix this," Griffin says, looking down at the pieces in his hand. "I write screenplays, I don't know the first thing about fixing electronics."

"Go out and by a new one then. I'm sure it will be *fine,*" I suggest before turning back to the Professor and Dr Cooke. "We have more important things to worry about. We need to go over the information we have for this new project."

"Can't we discuss it on the plane?" Griffin yawns. "I was hoping to have a rest before we have to leave for the airport."

"No, absolutely not," I say, shaking my head. "We

cannot discuss anything about this unless we are in a room with just the four of us. We cannot risk *anyone* overhearing us. If anyone else got wind of this it would be over before we started."

"Why is that?" Griffin asks.

"Because the bloody fool has no clue what he has," Dr Cooke says, taking his handkerchief out of his pocket and wiping his forehead. "Who sells a priceless artefact—even on the black market—for ten thousand pounds? We are talking about something that you couldn't even put a value on if you tried. He could ask for close to world and he would get it if the artefact is genuine."

"For just a ring?" Griffin asks, sitting up straighter at the mention of such fortune.

"My boy, this isn't just a ring!" the Professor says. "This is the lost ring of King Solomon. A ring belonging to the great King of Babylon which was inscribed with Jehovah's name. A ring that the wearer—when he *truly believed*—could do extraordinary things while in possession of it. The ring just as a historical piece from that era alone is priceless, when you add the story to the equation, well…"

"A ring that can do *what* sort of extraordinary things?" Griffin asks.

"There are many different theories. Muslims believe the bearer can control demons; other folklores say it could allow someone to communicate to animals–" I jump in.

"Wait a minute—*control demons?*" Griffin stands up. "I

don't know about this, June."

"Griffin, it's just a story," I say to him. "Obviously a ring cannot allow anyone to control things—spiritual or otherwise."

"Oh, I don't know, June," Dr Cooke says, pursing his lips. "As a historian, I'm not sure we should really be ruling anything out."

"Are you serious?" I turn to him.

"June, you yourself have studied many biblical artefacts. How can you unequivocally say that there is no power in that artefact?" he asks.

"Because... well... because a ring cannot *control* things," I say, shaking my head.

"Well, I guess we shall see, won't we?" Dr Cooke says, and the knowing tone in his voice makes me frown.

He doesn't honestly believe there could be any power in the ring, does he? I study Dr Cooke and realize that most of my worry has always been for the Professor, but Dr Cooke is just as much family to me. Perhaps it's time that I worry over his health the way I do with the Professor.

"Okay, so this bloke has a magical ring, and wants to sell it to you for ten thousand pounds?" Griffin shakes his head. "How did he even find you?"

"Through Simon," I explain. "I believe he has given his informant an—er—*incentive* to not reach out to other networks."

"So that's it?" Griffin asks. "We just have to go, see

the ring, and come home? That doesn't sound too bad."

"See, now that's the spirit!" I smile at him and turn to the others. "But we must remember not to talk about this in public. You never know who may be listening."

"My lips are sealed, June Bug," the Professor nods.

"Not a word," Dr Cooke crosses his heart.

I look at the two of them and know I'll be lucky if we get out of Britain before they cock this up.

Mrs Stevens makes her way into the room and I watch the Professor catch Dr Cooke's eye and put his finger to his lips, gesturing towards Mrs Stevens.

"You're all packed then?" she asks me and sniffs, not meeting my eyes.

Things have been a bit tense in the last forty-eight hours to say the least.

"Yes, thank you," I say, matching her stiff tone.

"Well, I suppose you will need these then," she says, handing me the bag of the Professor's medication.

My eyes widen. His medication might need a suitcase of it's own.

"Well, that's expanded quite a bit in the past few months," I say, studying all the bottles in the bag.

"Here's the list of times when the medication should be taken, and what he can and cannot eat before, after, or during each medication," Mrs Stevens says, handing me multiple sheets of paper.

"Right," I nod.

"It's important it is precisely followed," she says to me, and I see her cautiously flick her eyes in the Professor's direction.

She cares about him, it's obvious. I realize we don't see eye to eye on this trip, or all facets of the Professor's care, but I can tell she does have his best interests at heart. I soften towards her for the first time since our argument the other day and offer her a smile.

"I'll look after him," I say to her. "I promise."

"I'm sure you will try," she says tartly, and turns on her heels, leaving the room.

"That's a lot of medication," the Professor eyes the bulging bag and my list of directions.

"It's alright." My eidetic memory absorbs the list, determined to not miss even a single dose. "I'll make sure you get them at the proper times."

The Professor sighs, and I look up at him studying me.

"Have you ever considered that you might be fighting a battle which has already been won, June bug?" the Professor asks, peering over the top of his spectacles.

I study him for a moment before shaking my head.

"No," I say.

A small smile plays with the corner of his lips before he picks up the broken recorder from the bed. "That's my girl."

Chapter Three

"Once you've been in first class, you really can't go back," Dr Cooke says, stuffing complimentary packages of peanuts into Clint's bag as we exit the plane.

"Put this in there as well; it won't fit in mine," the Professor says, handing Clint the blue airline blanket.

Clint's ears turn red as his thin arm quickly stuffs the items into his bag. Honestly, he's going to have to learn how to say no to those two.

"You can't take those!" I hiss at the Professor, looking over my shoulder to see if anyone is watching us.

"Of course I can, they asked me if I wanted one," the Professor says. He hands Clint the white airline pillow next.

"Let's just find our driver," I sigh. I look around for anyone holding up a sign for us.

It's hard to see anything amongst all the people pushing past to make their way out of the airport. God, this lot would give the British tube commuters a run for their money. It's utter chaos in here.

"Oh, look! Palm trees." The Professor points to a long row of trees that have been lit with fairy lights and wanders off towards them.

"I'll go after him, then, shall I?" Griffin asks me, and before I have a chance to respond they're both gone.

"Er—I think they are supposed to be holding a sign with my name on it," I say, looking around again.

"Maybe they're outside?" Dr Cooke wonders, fanning himself with his hat. "By God, it's hot in this country."

"Oh, I think I see something," Clint points. His whole body is leaning heavily to the side as his tall, lanky frame tries to support the Professor and Dr Cooke's hand luggage.

"June?"

We all turn at the same time at the sound of a voice calling my name.

I make eye contact with the man and my shock renders me momentarily speechless.

"Thomas?" I ask, squinting at the man in front of me.

"I thought it was you!" Thomas offers me a wide smile. He's holding the hand of a beautiful, tall blonde woman who also offers me a smile.

"What—what are you doing here?" I stutter, and notice my voice is unusually high.

"We're on our honeymoon!" He turns to the woman beside him and beams. "Well, very *extended* honeymoon. This is our third stop."

I can't seem to manage any words, and swallow the huge lump that's formed in my throat.

"What are you doing here?" he asks, taking in Dr Cooke and Clint.

"I–"

"Found him," Griffin interrupts, coming to re-join the group with the Professor in tow. "Didn't get far, thank God."

I look at the Professor and the small rise of panic that has been building up in me seems about to explode.

The Professor looks at Thomas and instant recognition crosses his face. Of all the bloody things he manages to remember, of course it's Thomas.

"Thomas, my lad! How are you?" he asks, reaching for Thomas' hand.

I frown at the greeting and notice that Thomas hesitates only for a moment before shaking the Professor's hand.

"Haven't had you round for dinner in weeks," the Professor says, wagging his finger. "June's been keeping you all to herself again, has she?"

A slight crease of confusion clouds Thomas' face.

"Professor, I–" I start but the Professor ignores me.

"And you know Daniel, of course," the Professor says, pointing to Dr Cooke. "And, I'm not sure who the other two are…"

He looks at Clint and Griffin with innocent curiosity.

"This is Clint and Griffin, remember?" I say to him, trying to control the sudden heat in my cheeks.

The Professor completely ignores me.

"Daniel, you've met Thomas, haven't you? June's young lad. Very interested in the Anglo-Saxons and our excavation," the Professor smiles and winks at Thomas. "Always bending my ear for information. Can't get enough of my stories, can you?"

He laughs and looks at the woman standing beside Thomas.

"And who is your friend? Another history enthusiast?"

Thomas looks to me, confusion etched across his face.

"Er—this is my—friend—Carolyn," Thomas says, quickly glancing at Carolyn who also looks confused, but they both keep polite smiles in place.

"Oh, right. You better be careful, June Bug, she's a looker," the Professor says in a mock whisper to me and winks.

I have never wanted more in my life for the ground to open up and swallow me whole.

"Professor, Thomas and I aren't together anymore, remember?" I ask, putting my hand on his arm. "Carolyn is his wife."

The Professor looks at me for a moment before shaking his head.

"I don't think so," he laughs, and looks back to Thomas as though I haven't spoken. "You'll have to come around for tea this weekend. I want to show you some more of those excavation photos. I think I found the one with our tools you were asking about last week from the Sutton-Hoo site."

I clench my jaw at his words, but try and remain calm. My throat burns with painful memories.

Thomas avoids my eyes and smiles at the Professor.

"I'm sure that would be lovely," he says.

"Why don't I take the Professor and get our luggage?" Clint suggests, and for the first time since I've known him I want to hug him and never let him go.

"That is a *wonderful* idea," I say, trying to convey my gratitude.

"Come on Professor, let's go get the bags." Clint takes the Professor's arm and steers him towards the palm tree.

"He was always so welcoming," Thomas offers to me, I suppose trying to break the awkward silence.

"Yes, I'm sure he was," I say to him, trying to calm down my anger. "I'm sure his welcoming nature was very helpful when you were getting to know all about him."

We stare at each other and I forbid my chin to quiver even in the slightest.

"Right," he says, and nervously looks to the others. "Well, we better be going…"

"Yes, you should," I say and can feel Griffin frowning at my rudeness.

"I—well—it was nice seeing you again," he offers, taking his wife's hand. "Goodbye."

I watch as the two of them walk away, his wife leaning

towards him and speaking—perhaps asking what all of that was about.

"Er—did I miss something?" Griffin asks.

Dr Cooke quickly shakes his head at him, indicating for him not to press.

"Nothing," I say. "Let's go find the others."

"That didn't look like nothing," Griffin says. "Who was that guy?"

"He's no one that matters," I say, trying to navigate through the sea of people.

"The Professor said he was your lad," Griffin says and I turn around to face him.

"He was not *my* lad," I say to him, my hands on my hips. "He was a liar and a coward, but he was certainly not *my lad.*"

"Right," Griffin nods, his eyebrows raised.

I push my glasses further up my nose and exhale.

"We were friends, that was it," I say, shaking my head. "Did he lead me to think he wanted to be more? Perhaps. But it's not like *I* wanted to be more. I didn't even like him that much," I say in a frantic, high-pitched voice.

"I can see that," Griffin says.

"We met when I was just starting at Oxford and we went out a few times, that was all," I say, and can feel myself start to ramble. "I don't know where the Professor got the impression we were an item—because we were *not*. Yes, he came over to the house a few times—that doesn't mean we were going steady or anything. He didn't even want to go out with me anyways after... well, it didn't work out."

Griffin looks at Dr Cooke and frowns.

"What am I missing?" Griffin asks.

"That young chap was the one who sold the story that Albert had stolen the shield from our excavation of Sutton-Hoo to the papers," Dr Cooke explains, shooting an anxious glance in my direction.

"I thought *you* did that," Griffin says to Dr Cooke.

"I most certainly did not!" Dr Cooke bristles at the accusation. "The newspaper reached out to me and I declined to comment. Entirely different, my lad."

I shoot Dr Cooke an annoyed look, but choose not to comment.

"So he pretended to like June, got the information out the Professor, and sold it to the papers?" Griffin asks. "Did he know the Professor was not well?"

"It was still just speculation back then, but anyone close to him could see. He pretended not to know," I say, still seething at the memory. "At least, that's what he said after I gave him a black eye."

Griffin looks appreciative for a moment before shaking his head.

"That bastard. If I had known..." He clenches his jaw and looks over the crowd, obviously trying to spot Thomas.

"I know, it took everything inside of me..." Dr Cooke

scowls and the look of outrage on his face actually makes me laugh.

"What's so funny?" Dr Cooke asks.

"You… us… all here together," I say, shaking my head. "It has to be the smallest world."

My watch alarm beeps and I look down at it.

"It's time for the Professor's medication," I say, switching it off.

"Come on, let's go find the others, and our driver," Griffin says, taking my hand and leading me through the crowd.

"It's like bloody England," the Professor says in outrage, taking off his hat and banging it against his leg. "Where are the bloody pyramids?"

We step outside of the airport and look around at the tall buildings with paved roads. The skyscrapers shine in the bright sun, reflecting the rays off their silver mirrored surfaces.

"We were here in the eighties and it didn't look anything like this, did it Daniel?" the Professor asks.

"That was the seventies," Dr Cooke corrects.

"Our city has seen much growth, my friend." Our translator, Omar, smiles. "When we get out of the city, you will see the pyramids."

"I thought we would be travelling on camels," Dr Cooke frowns, looking at the white van parked in front of us. "That looks like something you would get abducted in."

Omar laughs joyfully while shaking his head. "It is much too far for camels, I am afraid."

"No pyramids, no camels. Should have bloody stayed in Britain," the Professor says, turning to Clint. "You said there would be sand."

"I—No, I didn't!" Clint says, dropping the suitcases by his feet and mopping his sweaty brow with his shirt sleeve. "And I am a part of the team now; I'm not supposed to be the one carrying all of your bags."

Clint straightens his slender shoulders, but then catches the Professor's hard stare and quickly shrinks.

"But, I guess I could still carry them..."

"June, what's that on your head?" the Professor frowns.

My hand automatically reaches up to my red, wide brimmed hat.

"What? My hat?" I ask.

"Where did you get that?" the Professor asks.

"Griffin got it for me for Christmas," I say, looking amongst the men all staring at me while my cheeks turn scarlet. "I just thought with all of the sun here, I'd wear it for a bit of a change instead of my brown one."

"It's very ostentatious." The Professor holds a hand up to shield his eyes as though the hat offends him.

"You have carnations in yours," I point out.

"Yes, but I have style," the Professor says..

I look to Griffin for support, but he is staring at all of the tall buildings, trying to take in his surroundings.

"Right, June, where are we going to buy this ring—" Dr Cooke starts.

"To visit our friend!" I quickly interrupt and shoot my eyes towards Omar. "We have a friend to visit."

"Very good," Omar bobs his head, still smiling. "I shall take you and your friends anywhere you like."

"Er—" I reach in my leather knapsack and take out the paper. "We need to go here. Do you know where that is?"

Omar frowns. "You have friends that live here, Ms Jenson?"

"Please, call me, June—and yes, why?" I ask, matching his frown.

His face clears and he is smiling once more. "If Ms June has friends here, then that is where I will take you."

I shoot Griffin a questioning look but he just shrugs and climbs in the van. Omar picks up some of the suitcases and starts to load.

"Right, in you go then Dr Cooke," I say, holding open the van door.

He climbs in and Clint follows close behind.

"I'll just make sure the driver puts my bag at the top," the Professor says. "Have a few valuables in there that I don't want damaged."

I raise my eyebrows and climb into the van, not wanting to know what he has smuggled into the country.

The less I know, the less I can be interrogated about at airport security.

Omar is very pleasant on the journey, keeping up a continual stream of touristy-style information about the city.

"We are the largest city in the Middle East, and expand all the way to the Giza pyramid," he nods at the Professor in the rear view mirror. "Our Arabic name: al-Qāhirah, meaning the Conqueror, was chosen because the conquering star of Mars was rising when our beautiful city was first discovered."

"There is quite a bit of traffic here," I comment, looking out the windows at the gridlock of cars all around us.

"Very busy, I'm afraid. We have a lot of armed police patrolling the streets, as you can see, which tends to slow car and foot traffic down. But don't worry, your friend doesn't live too far," Omar says, smiling.

I turn to catch Griffin's eye and he shoots a look in the direction of the Professor. I know he is thinking exactly what I am. The sooner we get there and get the ring, the less chance the Professor has of telling the world what it is we are doing here.

Chapter Four

"This is it?" I say, and take a step closer to Griffin.

"Your friend lives in that house," Omar says, pointing to the dilapidated row house in front of us. The stone steps leading up to the front door have sagged on the left side and look like they might crumble.

"Are you sure?" I ask, and look down at the piece of paper in my hand again.

"Very sure," Omar says, nodding.

"Er—alright then," I say, turning to look at the others. "Perhaps Dr Cooke and the Professor should wait in the car with Omar."

"Not bloody likely!" the Professor objects, fanning his face with his hat. "It's hotter in that van than the Sahara Desert."

"Well, I just don't know if he is expecting, er... so *many* of us," I say, shooting my eyes in Omar's direction.

"I'm not sure this bloke speaks English," Clint says, pulling out his notepad from his camera bag. "Simon didn't mention..."

"Let's not stand in the street," Dr Cooke says, clutching

his hat tightly to his chest while looking up and down the road. "I feel as if someone is watching us."

I look up and down the street as well. It seems to be the only area in Cairo in which I haven't seen a single policeman walking with a large gun in his hands. The thought is slightly unnerving.

"Nonsense," I say, forcing my voice to remain calm. "Alright, we'll all go, I suppose."

I look hesitantly to Omar, but realize it's no good—we will have to bring him along. If the man we are meeting doesn't speak English we will need him to translate. He was hired by Simon after all, so we must be able to trust him. At least to some extent.

"I don't like his," Griffin mutters.

"It'll be fine. Come on," I say, offering Griffin a smile.

We make our way up the concrete steps, and thankfully they are more stable then they look. The railing is another issue, but after it bows under my touch I quickly take my hand back and warn the others not to use it.

The black paint on the door is peeling to reveal a murky brown colour underneath. There isn't a doorbell or knocker so I raise my fist and knock on the door, hoping it's loud enough for someone inside to hear.

Nothing happens and I wait, staring at the door. After a few moments I raise my hand and knock again, a little more forcefully this time.

"Guess nobody's home," Griffin says from behind me.

"Oh well, back to England, I suppose."

I frown at him and turn to knock one last time. I raise my hand and knock once, lifting my hand to knock again but it is suddenly met with air as the door is jerked open.

"What the hell do you want?" the man who answers the door gruffly asks.

He's wearing a filthy shirt that I suspect was once white but now has so many yellow and brown sweat stains on it's hard to tell. His hair is a dishevelled mess, wiry brown mixed with grey. The stench of old alcohol on him makes me take a step back and raise my hand to my nose.

"Whatever it is you're selling, I ain't buying," the man says, spitting on the ground by my foot.

"You're American," I say, taking a deep breath before I lower my hand.

I ignore the sound of disgust that comes from the Professor at this revelation.

"And you're English," he says, scratching his exposed stomach. "Now that we have that sorted, get off my property."

"We're here—that is, Simon Locke asked us to come and see you." I let Simon's name hang in the air between us.

He raises his eyebrows.

"He did, did he?" the man asks, and studies me for a moment, looking me up and down.

"He said you might have something which would

interest us," I say to him, not wanting to say anything more in front of Omar now that I know we won't need him to interpret for us.

"Yeah, I might," he nods and looks at the others standing behind me. "They're all with you, are they?"

"Yes," I nod, and turn to Griffin, who looks like he might have stepped in something.

"Well, I guess you better come in then, hadn't you?" he asks.

I take a deep breath, preparing myself for what the inside of the place might smell like, and nod.

"Omar, would you be able to wait for us?" I ask, turning to look back at him.

Omar looks suspiciously at the man now picking dirt out of his nails.

"You do not wish me to stay with you? You may need my... assistance," he says.

"We will be alright," I reassure him with a soft smile.

"Well, are you coming or going?" the man says behind me, and I turn to look at him.

"Lead the way." I try to smile, and he turns to walk into his house.

The entryway consists of a small hallway. The walls, once painted white, now match their owner's shirt.

"Just through here," he says, walking through a doorway on the right.

I walk into the room and watch as he collapses into the

leather chair set up a few feet in front of an old television set. The only other furniture in the room is a tray table beside the chair, a mustard brown couch with springs protruding through the cushions, and a small curio cabinet under the window.

"Well, come in then," he says, and waves to the couch. "And make sure you shut the door!"

I hear the door close behind me and make my way into the room with the men following close behind.

"Well, are you just going to stand there?" he asks, his one leg draped over the arm of the chair.

"Er—you two sit," I say to the Professor and Dr Cooke.

The two men look suspiciously at the couch. The Professor takes out his handkerchief and places it on the far left couch cushion before carefully sitting down. Dr Cooke, watching the Professor, follows suit and sits next to him.

Clint looks from me to the pair of them and takes the last spot on the couch. Griffin leans on the doorframe.

"Look, Mr..." I prompt.

"The name is Quinn. So Simon asked you to pay me a visit then, did he?" Quinn asks, massaging his palm with his thumb.

"Er—he said you would have something that would interest us," I remind him.

God this is so out of my league. Should I just come out with it? Ask him if he has the ring? I look at Quinn as he stares at me, perhaps wondering which one of us will crack first.

"I might," he nods, not saying any more.

"God, it's bloody boiling in here!" the Professor says, wiping his brow.

"You're in Egypt, my friend," Quinn says, taking his eyes off of me to look at the Professor. "It's always boiling."

Dr Cooke takes his hat off his head and starts fanning his face.

"Well?" I hear from behind me, and turn to see Griffin stepping away from the doorway towards Quinn. "Do you have it or not?"

"You're not the poker player in the group, I take it?" Quinn asks and smiles for the first time.

"I just want to get what we came for and get the hell out of here," Griffin says, and cautiously looks around the room. "Well?"

Quinn looks from Griffin to me, still smiling, before slowly nodding his head.

"Yeah, I've got it," he says, and sits up in his chair.

The Professor raises his eyebrows and leans forward.

"You have Solomon's ring?" he asks, barely hiding his scepticism.

"You have the money?" Quinn asks me.

"Show us the ring, first," I say to him.

"That's not how it works, lady," he shakes his head. "I

see the money, or you don't see a goddamn thing."

I stare at him for a moment, weighing up my options.

"Okay," I say, turning to Clint. "Show him."

Clint looks nervously at me, before picking up his camera bag and unzipping it. He takes out his video recorder and places it on the ground.

"Wait a minute! No cameras!" Quinn springs up from his chair and takes a step forwards.

"I wasn't going to film anything, mate," Clint says, holding his hands up in defence. "The money is under my equipment."

"I don't want no goddamn cameras in my house! What are you, the police?" Quinn accuses, looking to me.

"No, we are with a production company," I try and explain.

He lunges for me and grabs my arms. "I don't want any cameras! Are you listening to me?"

I sense more then see Griffin at my side in seconds.

"Take your hands off of her!" Griffin says is a low voice. "Now."

Quinn looks at Griffin for a moment before slowly releasing his grip.

"Get out," Quinn says, and takes a step back.

"What? But the ring—" I start.

"I don't want to be on any sort of program," Quinn says, shaking his head. "I don't know anything, and I haven't seen anything."

"Please, you don't have to be on any program," I assure him. "We will not mention your name, you have my word."

He looks around at the others in the room before taking another step back.

"They didn't say anything about any cameras," he mutters.

"What exactly did Simon tell you?" I ask.

"None of your business, is it?" Quinn says to me. "He helps me out of a jam, I help him out in return."

"Right," I frown.

I'm not sure I like being a part of this. I look at Quinn as his eyes dart around the room and realize something very funny is going on here. I mean, I didn't really think this whole thing was on the up and up, considering we aren't meeting at a very reputable establishment like a museum or university. But this man... there is something very *uneasy* about him.

He walks back to his chair and takes a seat.

"No cameras," he says to Clint, holding up his finger in warning. "But slowly show me the money."

Clint's eyes are wide and I can't say I blame him.

I'm just not sure about this whole thing, and my instincts are telling me to get as far away from this man as fast as I possibly can.

But he might have the ring.

Can I walk away from this knowing I might be walking away from one of the most important artefacts I will ever see in my lifetime?

I bite the inside of my lip and sigh.

I nod to Clint who opens the bag to show Quinn the money at the bottom.

Quinn's nostrils flare as he looks at the money.

"Ten thousand pounds?" he asks.

Clint nods nervously.

Quinn exhales and stands up.

"Alright, I'll be back," he says and before he leaves the room he turns around. "Help yourself to something from the bar."

He points to the cabinet under the window before leaving the room and closing the door.

I let out the breath I was holding and slump a little.

"Right, Clarence, I'll have a brandy," the Professor says to Clint, leaning back in his seat.

"You are not to drink a bloody thing in that cabinet," I hiss at the Professor before turning to Clint. "Where the hell have you brought us?"

"Me?" Clint asks, shrinking under my narrowed eyes. "I'm just told to go and bring my camera, it's nothing to do with me!"

"Like hell it isn't," I spit at him. "You knew exactly what you were doing in Colorado, leading us around while pretending to be their intern; the whole time in Simon's pocket. Don't think for a moment I don't know you and Simon are all chummy. I bet you he told you exactly what type of a charlatan we were coming to meet here!"

"I—I never—he never," Clint sputters, his face growing red. He looks to the others for help. "I've been told exactly what you've been told."

"What sort of jam is Simon helping him out with?" I ask, taking a step towards him. "If this is anyway illegal, so help me *God*."

"Well it's not bound to be on the up and up, is it?" Griffin says from beside me.

I turn to look at him.

"Well, it's not, is it?" he argues, shrugging. "We are buying a priceless historical artefact, from a man who probably hasn't changed his shirt in a month, for ten thousand quid. What did you expect?"

"I—I don't know," I sigh, shaking my head. "Not this, though."

"Why does he want British pounds, anyways?" The Professor frowns. "Wouldn't he want American dollars?"

"Really? Is that what you are concerned with right now?" I ask, throwing my arms in the air.

"Let's just get the ring and get out of here," Dr Cooke interrupts and moves his leg strategically so that his trousers aren't touching anything but his handkerchief.

A sound at the door causes us all to turn.

"Right," Quinn says, coming through the door and walking towards me. "Here it is."

I look down at the envelope he holds out to me.

I carefully take it. With one last look at him I open it and see a small piece of paper inside.

"But, where's the ring?" I ask him.

"No clue," he says, shrugging. "But that will help you find it."

I frown.

"You said you had the ring," I argue.

"No, I didn't," he shakes his head. "I said I might have something that interests you."

"But—what is this?" I ask, holding up the envelope.

"A map to the ring," he explains, crossing his hairy arms over his chest.

"A map? To the ring?" I repeat, looking down at the paper. "How do you know?"

"I was told as much when I acquired it," he says. "Simon said you would be able to use that to find the ring."

I look around at the others in disbelief before turning back to Quinn.

"I can't bloody wander around Egypt following a treasure map, can I?" I hold up the envelope. "We don't exactly *blend* in here, do we? We'll be dead within the hour."

"That's what I have," Quinn shrugs. "If you don't want it, I have other people who do."

He reaches for the envelope and I pull it closer to my chest.

"What other people?" I ask him.

He shrugs.

"That's my business, isn't it?" he asks. "As I said, I'm doing Simon a favour. But if you don't want it…"

I look at the Professor and Dr Cooke who are watching the exchange with confusion.

I raise an eyebrow in Griffin's direction, asking his opinion.

"You can't be serious?" Griffin asks me, shaking his head. "We need to get out of here for Christ's sake."

Biting my lip, I look down at the envelope in my hand. Without waiting for anyone's approval I open it.

"Oh, I don't think so," Quinn says, snatching the paper out of my hand. "You see the paper when I get my money."

"How do I know you haven't just drawn nonsense on there," I argue.

"I guess you'll have to trust me," he smiles, exposing his stained teeth.

This is insane. I don't know why I am even considering this. It doesn't matter what is written on that paper, because I cannot do a single thing about it. I cannot run all over Egypt looking for some lost treasure I don't even know for certain exists. We would all be shot within the day, I'm certain.

Then again, if this information is genuine, Quinn will sell it to someone else. Someone with more questionable morals than Quinn, I'm sure. Can I leave this piece of history with a man who might turn around and sell it to someone who will damage it, or hide it away, in their own seedy private collection?

I study him for a moment before turning to Clint.

"Give him the money."

Chapter Five

"June!" Griffin yells, coming to stand beside me.

"It's just a piece of paper, which we can do with as we like," I reason, then add quietly: "I have to know."

Griffin studies me for a moment though doesn't say anything even though I can tell he doesn't agree.

Quinn walks over to Clint and hands him a bag, which I didn't see him carrying in his other hand.

"Put the money in there," he says to Clint.

Clint looks up at me, warily, but does as he is told.

"The paper," I say to Quinn, holding out my hand.

"A deal is a deal," Quinn says, handing me the folded piece of paper.

Just as I am about to open it there is a large bang at the front door.

"What was that?" Dr Cooke says, looking around terrified.

"Are you expecting someone else?" I ask Quinn, who looks just as nervous.

"No… well… no," he says, shaking his head.

The banging gets louder and I wonder if the person is

knocking or trying to break down the door.

"I'll just go see," Quinn says, and leaves us all to stare at the now closed door.

"We need to leave," Griffin hisses to us, gesturing for everyone to get up.

"How?" I ask, looking at the door and hearing the muffled voice of Quinn on the other side of it.

"The window," Griffin whispers and carefully pries open the window, trying not to make a sound. "Quickly!"

The Professor and Dr Cooke don't need asking twice and they quickly make their way over to the now open window.

"It's an eight foot drop!" Dr Cooke hisses over his shoulder at Griffin.

"Bend your knees when you land, Daniel," the Professor says knowingly. "That's what we were taught in the army."

"You were never in the bloody army!" Dr Cooke says in an angry whisper to the Professor.

There is a loud thump from behind the door and a scared cry.

"Out the bloody way!" The Professor says, and squeezes past Dr Cooke to drop out of the window.

Dr Cooke gives me one last frightened look before jumping himself.

"What about the money?" Clint asks.

"Leave it!" I say. "We don't want anyone chasing after

us for it."

He nods and picks up his camera, putting it back in his bag.

"June, hurry up!" Griffin says, and pushes me to the window. "Jump, we are right behind you."

I nod, tucking the paper quickly into the front pocket of my knapsack and slipping through the window as I hear another cry and the thumping of boots behind me.

I land hard on the cement ground. I feel a sharp sting in my palms from where the asphalt has scrapped them. Before I have a moment to think there is a loud thump beside me, followed by another and then Griffin's hand is under my arm pulling me up.

"Everyone quietly move up the alleyway," Griffin whispers, not taking his hand from my arm.

The Professor, limping slightly, is supported by Dr Cooke and Clint, and we slowly and very quietly make our way up the alleyway to where we left Omar with the car.

Griffin and I lead the charge, and when we make it to the corner of the buildings we peer around.

Whoever came to visit Quinn didn't bring a vehicle, as there are no cars outside of his house—including ours.

"What should we do?" I whisper to Griffin.

He holds his finger up to his lips.

"Listen," he whispers.

Raised voices travel down the alleyway from the open window we just jumped through.

"I don't have it all right now, but I'll get it," Quinn's frantic voice pleads. "Here's ten thousand pounds. It's all yours. You'll get the rest."

I hear a low reply but can't make out what the voice is saying.

"No, I promise, I'm good for it," Quinn says.

The low voice speaks again.

"There's no need for guns!" Quinn cries out.

My wide, frightened eyes meet Griffin's and he puts his finger to his lips again, reminding us to stay quiet.

"I'll get it, I promise. There's this ring. It's worth a bloody fortune. It was some King's. I know how you can find it."

I can't help the gasp that escapes me and I feel as though the piece of paper I just shoved into my bag is scorching lava.

"No, I'm not lying, I promise. There's this British woman, she has it. She knows where to find it," Quinn shouts.

I think I might actually be sick.

Suddenly I feel an arm on my shoulder and I jump what feels like fifty feet, ready to be attacked by whoever is holding Quinn at gunpoint.

But it is our driver, Omar, and he also has his finger to his lips. He gestures for us to follow him.

I look over my shoulder to make sure the Professor, Dr Cooke, and Clint are following, and then follow Omar onto the street. I am convinced that at any second men will burst onto the street and start chasing us.

"The van is down this street," Omar says, gesturing for us to keep up.

I keep my head down, trying to look inconspicuous to the few pedestrians on the street, but with the Professor limping I can feel we are attracting looks. Finally we see the van parked up ahead.

"Hurry up, get in!" Omar says, and quickly gets into the driver's seat himself.

I hold the door open as Dr Cooke and Clint help the Professor into the van. I take one last look up the street and freeze for a moment as a car drives past. My brain registers what it just saw, but I still frown, not quite believing it.

"June, quickly," Griffin urges and I climb in after the others with Griffin behind me.

"Oh my God," I say, and start to shake uncontrollably. "Oh my God, he told them who I am."

"It's alright," Griffin says, putting his arm around me, looking over his shoulder. "We are going to the airport. We are getting the hell out of here."

"The airport has been closed," Omar says, shaking his head. "There was a bomb threat and the government shut it down."

"I'm going to be sick," I say and start to hyperventilate.

"For how bloody long?" Dr Cooke yells from the back

seat.

"It could be hours, days, who knows," Omar shrugs.

"What are we supposed to do?" Griffin asks, and I can feel his hand on my shoulder start to quiver.

"Your hotel is safe; I will take you there and you can wait until the airport is reopened," Omar says.

"Griffin," I say, turning in my chair to gaze at him. "I think I just saw Thomas."

"What? Where?" he says, looking out his window.

"Back there, as we were getting in the van. You don't think—what do you think he was doing there?" I ask.

"No clue," Griffin shrugs. "It might not have even been him, could be someone that looked like him."

"Maybe," I concede, though my mind knows what it saw.

"Thomas is such a lovely lad," the Professor says from behind me. "You should bring him to tea on Sunday, June."

I ignore the Professor and lean forward towards Omar.

"Those men," I say, looking from Griffin to Omar. "Did you see the men who went into the house after us? Do you know who they are?"

"They looked like some of Gamal's men," Omar says, nodding. "I saw the big one before when Gamal was at a public event. I was interpreting for a dignitary who was one of Gamal's guests. The big one was part of Gamal's protection.

"Who is Gamal?" I ask.

"Ahmed Gamal," Omar explains. "One of the wealthiest men in Egypt. He has the government in his pocket. He's made his riches from oil."

"So what does he want with Quinn?" I ask.

"Ahmed Gamal is not a nice man. He is a business man, but most people know that he is a ruthless man who has, shall we say, *expanded*, his business practices," Omar explains.

"Oh God," I say, and feel the tears streaming down my face. "What do they want?"

"Money. Your friend must owe him money," Omar says, meeting my eyes in the rear view mirror.

"He is not my friend," I say to him. "The hotel where we are going, are you sure it is safe?"

"As safe as any place you can find in Egypt," Omar says.

"He doesn't know your name, June," Griffin says to me.

"What?" I ask.

"Quinn, he doesn't know your full name," Griffin says. "That will make it hard to find us."

"Griffin, how many British woman travelling with four men do you think there are in Cairo?" I ask him, shaking my head.

"I didn't say it was going to be impossible, I just meant it will take them some time to try and track you down.

That's if they even believe what Quinn told them."

"That's not very reassuring," I say.

"Well, unfortunately, it's all we've got until we can get out of here," Griffin says.

I turn to Clint.

"What name is the hotel reservation under?" I ask him.

"Er—mine, I think," Clint says, rummaging through his bag again and pulling out another sheet of paper with trembling hands. "Yes, it's under my name, a three bedroom suite."

I relax a fraction, then turn back to Griffin.

"We need to keep an extremely low profile; not draw any attention to ourselves. We should stay in the car until Clint has checked in. We don't want anyone to see us all together. We can go up to the suite in small groups," I instruct them. "Then when the airport opens we get the hell out of here."

"Hear, hear," Dr Cooke says, taking his hat off and using it to fan himself.

Chapter Six

"How could you?" I practically scream into the phone.

"June, calm down," Simon says from the other end and his condescending tone makes me want to throw the phone into the wall.

"Calm down? I might have the bloody Egyptian mob after me, and you want me to *calm down*?" I yell. "How could you send us here for a piece of paper? You said he had the ring, not a map to get it!"

"I knew you wouldn't go if I just said it was a clue," Simon confesses.

"You're right, and we are not bloody staying either," I say.

"June, I think you are overacting here," Simon sighs. "You've got an armed guard—"

"We've got one man!" I shout. "Was he the only one left, or did you get a discount?"

"He came highly recommended," Simon says. "And it sounds like he got you out of a bit of sticky mess—so, right man for the job, I'd say."

"I was only in a 'sticky mess' because your contact

owes money to some sort of Egyptian gang and he's now sent them after me," I say to him.

"Right, I'll definitely have a word with Quinn about that—"

"Oh, you be sure to do that," I snap. "Meanwhile, we are leaving as soon as the airport reopens."

"June, don't be so hasty! You are there, you have the clue, what harm will a little poking around do?" Simon asks.

"A little poking around?" I ask, flabbergasted. "Oh, I don't know. We're only in a bloody war torn country with armed police on every corner. Let me have a little *poke about* and I'll get back to you if I'm not dead, shall I?"

"June," Simon sighs, "of course we don't want you to do anything that puts your lives at risk. Surely there are places you can go in Egypt with Omar that you would be perfectly safe."

I take a deep breath.

"I will not put my grandfather and Dr Cooke in any more danger. Poor Griffin's been lying down since we got to the hotel. And Clint... well he had a bit of a cry when we first got here, but I've finally managed to calm him down now," I say.

I don't mention the fact I have been so busy calming everyone else down that I am still a bundle of nerves about ready to explode at any moment.

"I don't want you to be in danger, but... I mean, you are in Egypt. Can you not visit some attractions, maybe make the most of it and get *some* footage for the network?" he asks.

"No," I say, shaking my head.

There is silence on the other end of the phone for a moment.

"Have you looked at the clue?" he asks.

I snort, rolling my eyes.

"Of course I have. You just wasted ten thousand pounds, I'm afraid."

We studied it for ages when we finally got into the suite. Huddled around the coffee table where I laid out the delicate piece of paper, and stared for what felt like hours.

"What does it say?" Simon asks.

"It says 'Up' in Ancient Hieroglyphics," I reveal.

"I didn't know you could read hieroglyphics," Simon sounds surprised.

"I studied it in University one semester," I explain.

"Oh yes, that memory of yours," Simon says.

I don't say anything, and wait for him to speak.

"But, what does it mean?" Simon asks, and I can imagine the frown lines on his forehead.

"It probably doesn't mean a bloody thing," I say, slipping off my shoes and putting them in the corner of the bedroom by our suitcases.

"There has to be something to it," Simon says. "Quinn assured me it was genuine."

"Did he now? Well, I can't imagine Quinn not being

honest," I say, my voice dripping with sarcasm. "Some friends you keep, by the way."

"Well, he's technically not *my* friend," Simon says. "He's a friend of a friend."

"Oh, even better. So if he had killed us you wouldn't have been able to identify him in a line-up." I shake my head in disgust. "He could have been a complete lunatic!"

Actually, he wasn't far from that.

"June, I can assure you, I had him checked out," Simon placates. "My friend knows him quite well."

"Hmm… I'm sure your friend is just *charming*, if Quinn is anything to go by," I say.

"Actually he says he knows you as well," Simon says. "Charles Bringlett."

"Charles Bringlett?" I say, dumbfounded. "Oh this just keeps getting better and better."

Poor, deluded Charles. I really should have guessed he had his hand in this somewhere. Of course the same man who recruited me for a secret alliance– which never existed; and accused my grandfather of stealing the Shield of Quell—which he didn't; and tried to pretend like the whole thing wasn't really his fault—which it was; is behind this.

Oh God, if Griffin finds out we are here due to a tip from Charles he will go ballistic.

Griffin never really took to Charles, though I can't really blame him. Three years ago we were running for our lives, trying to solve the mystery of who stole the Shield of

Quell from the museum right out from under all of our noses, and it was entirely on Charles' orders.

To be honest, I've not entirely forgiven Charles either. I feel it's safe to say your friendship can never fully recover after one of the parties tries to send you to prison, knowing full well you are innocent, just to save their own skin.

But, that's just me.

"Charles has his ear to the ground, so to speak, and has proved very reliable for these little tip offs," Simon says. "He was the one who first mentioned to me you were looking for your own project before you went to Colorado."

Interesting. So the one time I spoke to Charles since the trouble at the Ashmolean and he turned around and sold the information to the papers.

And he wonders why I don't have him round for tea anymore.

"Oh, are you referring to the time when you deceived us all into thinking Clint was the Professor and Dr Cooke's intern, and had us secretly filmed?" I snarl.

"All's well that ends well, June," Simon laughs.

Right, I sense we are not going to see eye to eye on this.

"Where did Quinn get this paper from anyways?"

I look down at the piece of paper, which looks as though it might fall apart at the slightest touch. The torn piece looks like it has been ripped from the bottom of a book's page.

"Where he procures everything—in the market. Apparently he was following a wealthy man around, for er... business reasons," Simon pauses, and I roll my eyes. "He and another man were speaking of a ring, and Quinn thought they might have been referring to some jewellery they had on hand. Well, when Quinn bumped into him, the man had no ring in his pocket, just some money and that piece of paper."

I look down at the piece of paper again.

"And how does our noble Mr. Quinn know this piece of paper has anything do with the ring of Solomon?" I ask, holding it up to catch the light through the paper.

"Well the bloke he acquired it from made a rather large donation a few years back to the Egyptian Museum. Apparently he's pretty high up in the Egyptian social standings, but Quinn says he's a right piece of work. He has a lot of better stuff in his mansion than what he donated, but he donates to maintain appearances and keep the government off his back. The pieces are now on display next to the Tutankhamun exhibit, claiming to be relics from King Solomon's time," Simon explains.

"But, how do you know this paper has anything to do with the ring? It could just have been a random piece of paper in his pocket."

"I don't, but this bloke, Ahmed something, well Quinn was playing cards with some of his men a little while back and they mentioned something about a ring and how his boss nearly had it once, but lost something he needed to get it," Simon says, and I can hear him getting excited. "Well, Quinn put two and two together, didn't he? He couldn't very well sell the information to this Ahmed bloke because he was the one who he nicked it off, and well, he thought I might be interested in it."

"This Ahmed man," I say, gripping the phone so tightly my knuckles turn white. "You don't mean Ahmed Gamal, do you?"

"That's it," Simon says. "Have you met him? I'd steer clear if I were you, June."

"I'll keep that in mind," I say, and sink into the chair.

"Listen, I know I've put you into a bit of a tricky spot here," Simon says, putting on a coaxing tone. "But listen, if you could just go to the museum, perhaps have a look around, and get some footage. I will speak to the curator, we'll get the permission for you. All you have to do is throw about some theories, and we'll edit and make what we can of it."

"Simon, I cannot do this," I whisper, putting my hand to my forehead. "I just—Quinn's told those men who I am."

"You've got Omar, and the museum is full of armed guards. You cannot pick a safer spot!" Simon argues. "Listen June, you do this and we will make it more than worth your while."

"What are you talking about?" I ask.

"You get me a decent theory to go along with this clue, some footage of the museum and donated artefacts, and we will do the rest," Simon says. "The Professor and Dr Cooke can retire with not a care in the world. We will take care of anything they need. Your boyfriend can have carte blanche for any theatre production he wants performed. And you—well, whatever you want June. A teaching position, a new career path, or perhaps a show entirely on your own... We have all the right connections and we will take care of you."

"But, the paper means nothing," I say, studying it again.

"It only means nothing if people *believe* it means nothing. People can thrive on theories for years, June. And something like this will cause a sensation. The networks ratings will go through the roof; we stand to make *millions* on this segment."

"Millions?" I say, raising my eyebrows.

"It's one day at a guarded museum," Simon says, and I can hear the smile in his voice. "What could possibly go wrong?"

Chapter Seven

"I don't like this," Griffin mumbles as we walk through the entryway to the Museum of Egyptian Antiquities.

"So you've said a million times," I snap at him. I take a breath to calm down. "Look, let's just get on with it and go home."

"I don't know why you are even bothering," Griffin says, shaking his head. "You don't owe them a bloody thing June. Look at what they've sent us into."

I don't respond, because I don't want to tell Griffin why we are doing this. If I told him it was to ensure the Professor has a comfortable retirement, or so Griffin can go back to doing what he loves to do, I know he would stop me. All of them would. They would selflessly hide me away until the airport reopened and we could go back to Britain. But I'm the one that got us all into this mess, and I'm going to be the one to get us out of it.

"It should just be through here," I say, leading the group through the Tutankhamun exhibit.

"Ms Jenson," a young Egyptian woman greets me at the entrance to the Tanis exhibit and reaches for my hand.

"Welcome."

"Thank you," I say, returning the smile.

"We have the whole area reserved for you today," she says, and turns to release one side of the heavy maroon rope stopping anyone from entering into the room.

"We very much appreciate it," I say to her, and walk past to enter the exhibit.

My eyes automatically start scanning the room, taking in the five different areas with artefacts displayed.

"And were you able to sign in at the front desk and complete the journalist orientation?" she asks, her hands carefully folded in front of her sharply pressed blue suit.

"Yes, we did, thank you," I say, nodding.

I think back to the section which said we would be spending our remaining years on the inside of an Egyptian jail cell if we touched or damaged anything, and shoot the Professor a quick glance.

It's a good day today. He's very alert, and actually seemed eager to get here while Omar was driving. Granted it might have been the fact the fan broke in the car and it turned the inside into a sweatbox.

"Will you need anything else?" she asks, and eyes the Professor suspiciously as he leans very closely to the Pharaoh's funeral mask, displayed on top of a large marble pedestal.

"No, we've got everything, thank you," I say.

"I will be downstairs if you need me," she says, and

with one last look in the Professor's direction, she turns and leaves.

"Right," I say, turning to Clint. "Shall we get set up?"

"Just need to turn the camera on," Clint shrugs as he takes the video recorder out of his backpack. "Takes two seconds."

He points to the button on the camera to show me.

"Don't you have some sort of a tripod?" I say. Honestly, I feel if I'm putting my life on the line it should at least look professional.

"Simon said he wanted a more candid shoot with this one, so no tripod," Clint says.

"Alright," I say, turning to look around the room again.

"Remind me again what this has to do with King Solomon," Griffin says, peering over the roped off display of the funeral cups. "Aren't these from some dead Egyptian Pharaoh?"

"Two Egyptian Tanis Pharaohs, who happened to reign and die around the same time as the reign of King David and King Solomon," I say, coming to stand beside him.

"So you think they could be the same people?" Griffin asks, as Dr Cooke and the Professor make their way over to stand beside us.

"It's possible," I nod. "There are quite a few theories that support it."

"More than *possible*, June," the Professor says, peering over at the funeral bowls. "These belonged to a Pharaoh who came into power during an impoverished era—who turned Egypt into one of the most wealthy, prosperous regions the world has ever seen."

"Right, and what does that have to do with King Solomon?" Griffin asks.

"My boy, did you never go to Sunday school?" Dr Cooke asks.

"I went," Griffin says. "Well, at Christmas and Easter."

"Hold on, I think I should be getting this," Clint says, lifting his arm and turning the camera on.

"King Solomon was the son of King David," Dr Cooke explains.

"He killed Goliath," Griffin interjects, obviously proud he knows something on the subject.

"Yes, David killed Goliath. He also had a son named Solomon," Dr Cooke explains. "Now, Solomon inherited the Kingdom from his father in less than favourable conditions. But God looked favourably on Solomon. When he came into power God told Solomon he could have anything his heart desired. Solomon, the great King that he was, asked for understanding and discernment. This pleased God greatly, because he did not ask for worldly possessions, but things that would bring Solomon closer to God and make him a better King. Because of the selfless act, God granted Solomon his heart's desire, but also bestowed on him great riches and honour."

"I used to do that with Mum," Griffin laughs, shaking his head. "Always asked for fruit, and she was so pleased she'd slip me a chocolate bar and tell me I was a good boy."

I smile in spite of myself.

"Yes, well, King Solomon prospered greatly and so did the people whom he ruled over. He was the first King to build a temple to store his riches, among which is believed to be the Ark of the Covenant," Dr Cooke says, and I can see he has made sure his best side is angled towards the camera. He smooths down the front of his waist coat.

"Wait—are you talking about the Holy Grail?" Griffin says, and quickly looks to me. "Do you think we might find that?"

"I don't think so," I say, laughing at the eagerness etched on his face. "We are in the wrong country, I'm afraid. It is believed the Knights Templar moved the Ark during the holy crusade. A priest found a manuscript in France which has led archaeologists and treasure hunters alike to believe it is buried there, but no one's found it yet."

"Another day, perhaps," Griffin smiles.

"Perhaps," I smile back.

"So King Solomon was rich, had God's favour," Griffin says, looking around the room. "What does that have to do with all of this?"

"Well the good King had vices as well," Dr Cooke says.

"And what was that?" Griffin asks.

"Women," Dr Cooke answers, winking at the camera.

"So the King got around, did he?" Clint grins from behind the camera.

I roll my eyes, and decide to step in before the boys' club work up steam.

"He fell in love, again and again. He had hundreds of wives," I say.

"Think of the alimony," Clint says and whistles through his teeth.

"There wasn't such a thing back then," I explain. "Besides, even if there were, this man could have afforded it. The real problem lay in the fact that he went outside of Egypt for love, and the women eventually led him to worship false Gods."

"Women, they'll be the death of us. Am I right?" Clint asks, flashing a cheeky grin to Griffin.

We all stare at him, and his smile falters.

"Er—so what does this all have to do with that ring?" Clint asks, looking around the room.

"That's the problem—nothing," I say, shaking my head. "The paper says the word UP in hieroglyphics, and was clearly ripped from a book, but there are no books in here," I say, looking around at the room. "It could be from anything, we don't even know if it has to do with the ring."

"Look here," Griffin calls, from the far corner of the room. *"Donated by Ahmed Gamal to the People of Egypt*—he's a real saint isn't he? Donated a bloody rock."

"It's a petroglyph," I correct, coming to stand beside

him to study the granite slab. "That's what it's called when people used to chisel pictures into stone to record history."

"Well, I'm sure he wasn't about to donate any of the gold he found, was he?" Griffin says, studying the pictures on the rock. "What does it mean?"

"It is describing the invasion of the Tanis Pharaohs," the Professor comes to stand beside it, tilting his head slightly as he studies the carvings. "You see, Egypt was going through a terrible civil war at the time, divided by North and South. The two armies met, here, in the Middle East to fight over the right to rule Egypt."

The Professor reaches out his hand where the two men face each other with weapons held over their heads.

"Here they are describing the famine the people of Thebes suffered during the civil unrest. The Nile was the main source of transporting supplies, but during war it was unsafe to use this means of travel." The Professor's hand traces the wavy lines etched on the stone with the small boat sitting crooked on top.

We stare at the small boat, and for a moment I can almost imagine the little boat moving on the choppy water.

"So do you think this Ahmed Gamal might still have the book?" Griffin asks me. "The paper only said 'UP', it's not a very hard clue to remember. Why do you reckon he hasn't found the ring yet himself even without the piece of paper?"

"Maybe he didn't know how to read ancient

hieroglyphics and lost it before he could have it translated. Remember, Quinn said Ahmed's men mentioned Ahmed had a chance to get the ring, but *lost* it," I say.

"This is all fascinating," Dr Cooke says, wiping his brow with his handkerchief. "But doesn't help us find the lost ring—if it even exists."

"And let's not forget who gave us this so-called *clue*: a bloody American," the Professor scoffs. "I need a cup of tea."

He turns and strolls out of the room.

"I'll go after him," Dr Cooke says, and quickly follows after the Professor.

Griffin and I stroll back over to the funeral display. The death mask that could have belonged to King Solomon himself is beside the display of bowls. Made of solid gold, the full lips and wide, long nose with large well spaced eyes combine to make a youthful face. Though, most likely the wearer would have been a senior when he died.

"And what were these used for," Griffin says, leaning closer to study the engravings. "Some sort of fancy soup bowls?"

The funeral bowls displayed on a white marble podium are exquisite, their intricate etchings highlighted by the stark contrast of the solid white stone. The first is silver with a herringbone pattern, which gets tighter towards the golden centre medallion. The second is also silver, but at the centre is a large gold ring with swirls that give the effect of liquid gold that is constantly moving. The last bowl is made of pure gold with a bevelled medallion at its centre.

"They were funeral bowls; they housed the embalming liquid used to dehydrate the body," I explain.

Griffin quickly stands up straight and swallows.

"How much longer are we going to be here?" Griffin asks, shifting his weight to his other leg. "I just don't know what you expect to find—"

He stops and we both turn at the sound of footsteps entering the exhibit.

Thomas walks in, his arm wrapped around his wife's petite form; her high heels click with every step.

I look to Clint and gesture for him to lower the camera.

"Thomas? What are you doing here?" I ask, my forehead creasing as I study him.

"Carolyn and I were just touring the museum," he smiles, looking around the room where we are standing. "Are you having a private viewing? I saw the ropes blocking off the exhibit."

He points to the heavy velvet ropes slung between two heavy brass pillars, one of which has been moved to the side to create a gap.

"Yes, and we would like to keep it private," Griffin says.

"That's right," Clint says bravely, holding his camera against his chest.

I look at him, raising my eyebrows at his forceful tone,

and look back to Thomas and raise my chin in solidarity.

"We didn't mean to intrude," Thomas says in apology, though doesn't move to leave. "I mentioned the Tanis exhibit to Carolyn while we were looking at Tutankhamun and she mentioned she would like to see it."

Carolyn looks at me, still smiling.

"Well, I'm sorry but this area is closed today. We're filming," I explain, pointing in Clint's direction.

"Are you doing a story on the Pharaohs of Egypt?" Thomas asks, his head tilting to the side with curiosity. There's just something a little forced with his casual tone, and my eyes narrow onto his.

"You're here for the story, aren't you?" I ask, shaking my head while smiling. "Have you been following me since the airport? Figured I was in Egypt for something, and thought you would shadow me in the hopes of getting the scoop?"

"What are you talking about?" Thomas laughs as though the idea is ludicrous.

"I should have known you would do something like this. Are you two even married?" I look at his wife who is frowning at me.

"Of course we are," she says, turning with a confused expression to Thomas.

"You were in the South end of Cairo yesterday, I saw you," I say, pointing my finger at Thomas.

"Yes, we were on a city tour," Thomas says calmly,

though I can tell from his rapidly blinking eyes that I am getting to him.

"What's your angle?" I ask him, tilting my head. "Are you here for your own story, or are you following me in the hopes I might give something up?"

"Really, June," Thomas laughs. "You sound paranoid."

"When a dog bites you once, you're not likely to stick your hand in its mouth again, are you?" I ask him. "I've followed your career: investigative journalist for the BBC focusing on historical discoveries. Now you must tell me—do you con all of your sources in order to get the information out of them, or did you reserve that especially for your big break?"

Thomas' eyes narrow fractionally, but he shakes off the animosity with a laugh.

"Honestly June, I don't know why you keep harping on that. You and the Professor were *cleared* from that unfortunate situation—my piece might have actually helped."

"*Unfortunate situation?*" I repeat incredulously. "You used me and my grandfather to further your career. You never gave a toss about us."

"That's not true, June," Thomas says and then catches the eye of his wife who is watching him with raised eyebrows. He pauses, and then smiles. "Listen, we've both moved on—grown up, if you will. You have a thriving career now—I've followed your work as well, fascinating stuff."

I stare at him and cross my arms over my chest.

"We might be able to help each other out, you and I," Thomas goes on, shrugging. "If you wanted to let me in on what you are doing here, we could cover it together, perhaps. I know your contract is coming to an end with your network—I could reach out to the BBC for you, put in a good word..."

"How do you know anything about my contract? Did you come to Egypt to follow me?" I ask him.

Thomas pauses, obviously weighing his answer.

"The BBC are fascinated with your excavations, June. Your viewership is great, and my director would love the chance for us to team up," Thomas says.

"You aren't on your honeymoon, are you?" I accuse, looking to Carolyn and willing her to respond.

"Carolyn supports my ambitions," Thomas says, looking at his wife and offering her a smile, which she promptly returns. "We were in Thailand when I got the call. The BBC saw your team was booked on a flight here, and considering our past friendship, asked if we wouldn't mind making a slight detour on our honeymoon."

"A slight detour," Carolyn gives a sing song laugh. "That's a journalist for you, isn't it? Also putting a rather creative spin on things."

She winks at me as though we are somehow comrades.

"I'd say," I give a mock laugh of my own. "Our *past*

friendship? You proposed to me, and the next week I find out you used me and my grandfather to get your big break in journalism!"

"You were *engaged* to him?" Griffin asks incredulously, and I jump at the sound of his voice.

Honestly, I forgot he was here.

"I—" I start, and then shake my head. "That's not important."

"Oh, I'm sorry," Griffin says, his voice dripping with sarcasm. "I just thought that might have been something you would mention. You know, I tell you I used to take tap dancing lessons; you mention you used to be engaged..."

He looks at Clint, who looks nervous, but offers a consolatory nod.

"Can we take about this later?" I say to him through clenched teeth.

"Of course, please, don't let us intrude," Griffin raises his hands in mock apology.

"Look, Thomas, I am not going to be sharing *any* sort of information or story with you, so you might as well go back to Thailand," I say. "Because if you think—"

I stop suddenly when the Professor, followed closely by Dr Cooke, enters the room.

"There you are!" the Professor says to me, shaking his head. "I've been looking everywhere."

"We've been here the entire time," Griffin points out.

"Are you our tour guide?" the Professor asks Griffin,

tilting his head to one side.

I frown, looking between the Professor's blank face and Griffin's look of concern.

"Er—no, it's me. Griffin," he says, taking a step closer to the Professor.

The Professor continues to look at him blankly before turning his gaze to me.

"Ah, June, there you are! Been looking everywhere for you," the Professor says, rubbing his hands together. "I've found a husband for you!"

My eyes widen and I feel the heat in my cheeks as the Professor turns behind him and beckons a young Egyptian lad in his early twenties forward.

I look at Dr Cooke who shakes his head.

"I tried to stop him," he offers.

"This here is Karim, he plays the clarinet and would love to become a British citizen," the Professor says, grabbing Karim's arm and pulling him forward.

Karim looks nervous, his dark eyes almost the same colour as his black hair.

"I like the English," Karim nods eagerly. "We can go there now, yes?"

I blink a few times while my brain tries to process.

"Er, Professor," Griffin says, taking a step forward. "June can't marry Karim. We are together, remember?"

The Professor looks from me to Griffin and relaxes into a smile.

"Are you? Well, that's wonderful!" The Professor says, clasping his hands together. "Will you marry her then? Only she had her heart broken not too long ago, and I know she's desperate to get married."

"I am not!" I say, my voice coming out in an absurdly high-pitched tone.

I clear my throat and turn to look at Griffin, forcing my voice to be calm.

"I am not," I repeat when Griffin looks at me warily.

I look to Thomas, who looks at me with pity and it's the last straw.

"I do not *have* to get married. I have a wonderful, thriving career," I say to no one in particular.

"And a wonderful boyfriend," Griffin adds, sardonically.

"Yes of course," I say, placing my hand on his arm.

He offers me a sideways glance but doesn't say any more and I turn back to Thomas.

"You certainly didn't break my heart. My life is wonderful, I count myself lucky everyday I never ended up marrying you. No offense," I add, looking at Carolyn.

"And who are you?" the Professor says, looking Clint up and down. "Are you filming something? I love television."

"Right, we are leaving," I announce to the room, picking up my knapsack from beside my feet.

"We go to England?" Karim asks Dr Cooke.

"Er—no, I don't think so," Dr Cooke says, taking Karim's arm. "Let's get you back to your family, shall we?"

The two leave, Karim frowning at Dr Cooke, and I turn to Clint.

"Do we have all the equipment?" I ask in an overly friendly voice, my cheeks still flaming scarlet.

"Er—yes," Clint says, holding up his camera and bag for me to see.

"Right, well," I turn back to Thomas and his wife, and lift my chin. "You have my answer, so I suppose this is the last time we will see each other. Good luck."

I nod to both of them and stroll past the group, trying with all my might to stop my legs from shaking.

Chapter Eight

"Some people are so bloody inconsiderate," the Professor says, slouching down further on the couch. "Setting off a bleeding bomb at the airport—no thought for those of us that haven't had a proper tea and scone in *days*."

I count to ten, willing myself not to snap at him.

They are driving me up the bloody wall, the lot of them.

I just don't think it's healthy to be locked inside a small area with your family for four days without being able to go outside for some sanity. There really should be a law against it.

"Two days," Griffin slams the phone down, shaking his head. "Two more days until it's open!"

"I'll have melted by then," Dr Cooke moans, fanning himself more vigorously with a newspaper.

"There's central air in here," I argue, frowning. "And, you're wearing a sweater!"

"It's no good trying to make me feel better, June," Dr Cooke says, putting his hand to his forehead.

"It's all this sun," the Professor says, shielding his eyes from the sun's glare through the window. "Does it never bloody rain here?"

"Should I close the blinds?" Clint half rises from beside the Professor, eager it seems, for anything to do.

"No point, I still know its there," the Professor says, shaking his head.

I decide to count to twenty instead.

"Why don't we do something a little productive?" I say, hoping to distract them. "We haven't watched the footage yet that Clint filmed."

"I don't see the point," Dr Cooke sighs. "Complete and utter waste of time."

I stare at the pair of them and start taking deeper breaths.

Honestly, it's not like I'm having the time of my life here.

"Well, I'd like to watch it," I say, forcing cheerfulness into my tone. "Griffin?"

I look at Griffin, who looks beyond bored, and he simply shrugs.

"That's the spirit," I say, and turn to Clint. "Why don't you put it up on the television for us all to watch, Clint?"

He looks as though he is about to argue, but decides better of it, and gets up to get the camera.

The sharp sound of my watch's alarm makes everyone in the room jump.

"Right, time for your medication," I say to the Professor and fish in my bag for the allotted dosage.

"I'm not taking that," the Professor says, shaking his head. "I'd rather forget this, if it's all the same to you."

"Tough luck," I say, forcing the pills into his palm. "If I have to remember this, then you do as well."

He studies me for a moment and I can tell he is debating whether to kick up a fuss. I narrow my eyes at him, and after a moment he gives in and tips the pills into his mouth.

"Excellent," I say, nodding. "All ready to go, Clint?"

"It's only one cord," he shrugs, sitting down between the Professor and Dr Cooke with the small remote which controls the camera.

The blue screen suddenly switches to my image, and I begin to talk about the Pharaohs of Egypt. Clint managed to get pretty decent shots of the artefacts that were on exhibit yesterday before he pans to Dr Cooke who begins his background story of King Solomon.

"My hat shows beautifully on camera, and look at that jaw line," Dr Cooke proudly boasts, pointing to the screen. "I inherited that from my Great Uncle Isaac. He was in Parliament, you know."

"Your great uncle was a bloody chimney sweep," the Professor snorts.

"That was my Great Uncle John! Isaac was in Parliament," Dr Cooke sniffs, lifting his nose in the air.

The Professor looks doubtful and opens his mouth to say something else, but Griffin shushes them.

"This is my part!" he says, as the camera pans to him studying the petroglyph. "Clint, you idiot! You've only got me from the neck down! You can't even tell who is speaking."

Griffin looks to Clint whose ears turn pink.

"The camera cord got stuck on my shirt button," Clint says, the blush highlighting his freckles.

"It's funny, there's just something about that boat; the way they carved it," I say, tilting my head. "My eye is so drawn to it, it looks as though it is moving along the water, doesn't it?"

At that moment the phone rings, and Griffin gets up to answer it, still glaring at Clint.

"Hello?" he says, turning his back to us to block out the sound of the television.

"They had remarkable artistic talents," Dr Cooke says to me in agreement. "To think they had the most modest, barbaric tools with which they could carve such detail."

"What, when?" I hear Griffin shout into the phone, then turns to look at me, a worried look on his face.

"What is it?" I say, standing up.

Griffin holds up a finger, telling me to wait a moment.

"Right, and you think they are coming up?" he asks to the person on the other end.

"Okay, cheers," he hangs up the phone and looks at me. "We have to leave."

"Why, what's happened?" I ask, following him into the

bedroom as he starts throwing our stuff into the suitcase.

"I think they've found you," Griffin says, not stopping for even a moment.

"Gamal's men?" I ask, my eyes widening in fear.

Griffin nods.

"Clint, call Omar! We need him to come and pick us up right now. And pack up your stuff, we have to leave," Griffin yells into the other room.

"How do you know?" I ask Griffin. Dr Cooke and the Professor come to the bedroom door to listen. "How do you know his men are here?"

"I booked a room under the Professor's name three floors below and paid the front desk to tell me if someone came looking for the room number," Griffin says, not breaking his stride as he enters the bathroom and unceremoniously clears the contents on the counter into the smaller suitcase.

"Why *my* name?" the Professor asks, outraged.

"Because once they found out June's name it was only a matter of time before they started tracking her down," Griffin explains, coming out of the bathroom. "They would have first called and asked if any British women were registered for a room. Putting it under your name instead of one of ours tells us they know her last name."

"Griffin that was..." I say, looking at him slightly dumbfounded. "That was brilliant."

Griffin pauses for a moment, grinning.

"It was, wasn't it?" he agrees and then shakes his head, coming to back to reality. "We don't have much time. Once they figure out we aren't in the other room they are bound to ask around and I'm sure one of the bellhops or maids will let our actual room number slip for a few quid."

"Right, you two—pack!" I yell to the Professor and Dr Cooke. I run around the room and help Griffin throw our stuff in the suitcase.

I just finish zipping up the suitcase when the Professor strolls in the room, his humidifier in his hands and his trousers off.

"Has anyone seen the bloody cord?" he asks, scanning our room.

"Leave it!" Griffin says, grabbing the humidifier out of his hands and ushering him out of the room. "I'll sort them out, June, you check to make sure we have everything.

I nod and then stand up straight.

The clue. It's in the safe.

I run over to the wall safe, and enter the code.

Access denied.

What the bloody hell?

"June, they're all packed," Griffin says, putting his head through the door. "We have to go."

"Go and get the Professor to the car," I say, waiting for the little words to disappear from the screen so I can re-enter the code.

"I'm not leaving you!" Griffin says, running over to me.

"What's wrong?"

"The safe won't open and the bloody machine is taking forever to let me have another go," I say, tapping my foot and staring at the little screen.

"Leave it!" Griffin says, trying to pull my arm.

"I can't!" I yell, yanking it back. "Not only is the clue in there but so are our passports!"

"Omar is outside," Clint says, popping his head through the door.

The screen finally resets and I carefully put the code in again.

Access denied.

What the hell is going on?

"Look, go and take the bags down with the Professor," I say, frustration making my tone clipped. "It won't do us any good to stroll out to the car in a large group anyways. We'll blend in better if we split up."

"I said I'm not leaving you," Griffin says through clenched teeth.

"We don't have time to argue, I'll be down in a minute with Clint," I say, to him. "Please—I need to make sure the Professor is safe; you're the only one I trust with him."

"And who is going to make sure you are safe?" Griffin asks.

"Clint and I will be right behind you," I say, and give him a chaste kiss before returning my attention back to the safe.

I can feel his gaze on me for a moment, and then he turns around and walks over to Clint.

"Under no circumstances do you leave her behind," Griffin warns him and turns back to me. "I will see you downstairs in one minute or I'm coming back up for you."

"Go!" I say to him, but shoot him a quick wink.

He smiles briefly and then disappears behind the door frame.

I turn my attention back to the safe, carefully re-entering the code and waiting...

Access denied.

"This bloody piece of crap!" I say, smacking my hand on the side of safe.

"What's wrong?" Clint says, coming to stand beside me.

"It won't open!" I say.

"Just leave it!" he says and glances at the door, obviously not too pleased he isn't leaving with the others.

"I can't! The clue is in there with our passports," I say, my hand still smarting from hitting the rock hard safe. "We'll never be able to get out of the country."

"Ugh, out of the way!" Clint says, pushing me aside. "What's the code?"

I reel off the number.

"Are you sure?" he asks.

"Of course I am, it's my password for everything. It spells JUNE," I explain.

"Well, that's not very bright," he says, rolling his eyes.

"Why not?" I ask.

"It's not particularly hard to crack, is it?" he asks. "Did you press the pound button when you were finished typing in the code?"

"Of course I pressed—oh," I say, pursing my lips. "Actually I forgot that bit."

He presses in the code followed by the pound symbol and the latch releases at once.

I reach inside and take out the small piece of paper and passports.

"See June, technology like so many things, is only as good as the user," Clint says, taking a step back.

"Let's go!" I say, ignoring his comment.

We run out of the bedroom and through the living room towards the door.

"My camera!" Clint says, halting in mid stride, causing me to run into him. "It's still hooked up to the television!"

I watch as Clint sprints over to the television and picks up his camera.

I look at the television screen, on the image of the petroglyph and the little boat. Again it looks like it is a second away from going over the little wave and I finally see what it is that intrigues me about the little ship.

"Wait! Stop!" I yell, holding up my hands.

"What? What's wrong?" Clint asks.

"The boat," I say, running over to the television,

putting my face inches from the screen. "It's there! On the boat's stern! It's the hieroglyphic!"

I look at Clint in wonder.

"Do you know what this means?" I ask him.

"Not a bloody clue," Clint says, and yanks the cord out of the television and shoves the camera into his bag. "Come on!"

We tumble into the hallway, and run over to the elevator.

"It's rising!" Clint says, pointing to the numbers above the elevator doors. "They are coming up here."

"The stairs," I say, grabbing his hand and dragging him over to the door leading to the stairwell.

I push Clint through and hear the chime of the elevator just as the stairwell's door closes.

"Quickly!" I hiss, motioning him to start going down the stairs.

We begin to run down the stairs, both out of breath after ten flights.

"How much further?" Clint pants as we turn down another flight.

"Six more levels," I say, clutching the stitch in my side.

"Are they following?" he asks, not looking up or breaking pace.

"I don't think so, but don't stop!" I try to keep up with him.

We finally make it to the lobby, both of us panting.

"We've got to look casual," I say to him, gasping for breath. "Just look straight ahead and don't draw attention to yourself."

Clint looks petrified, but I don't have any time to talk him up to this. Instead I grab his hand and yank open the door with my other.

The lobby is sleek marble with minimal furniture to hide behind, but luckily there is hardly anyone around.

"Where's the van?" Clint hisses.

"It will be there," I whisper back.

"Can I help you with anything, miss?" a woman wearing a black suit with the hotel's insignia on the pocket appears out of nowhere, making Clint and I jump.

"Er—no thank you," I say, stepping around her. "We are just stepping out for a bit."

I don't wait for her to say anything else, instead tugging Clint's hand to keep him moving.

We get to the large glass entry doors and look outside, but the van isn't in front of the hotel.

"Where is it?" Clint says, his voice on the brink of hysteria.

"I don't—" I stop when I hear the door for the elevator open and see three men step out and begin to scan the lobby.

"Quickly, over here," I say, tugging Clint so we are half hidden behind one of the large palm trees lining the lobby's glass windows.

"Oh God, they're going to find us," he whispers, the panic evident in his voice.

And he's right, they certainly will with us standing here half hidden behind the palm tree. It looks like we are trying to hide because why else would a man and a women be leaning up against a large tree?

Unless...

"Just go with it," I say, when the spark of inspiration hits me.

I see Clint frown, but I don't stop to explain as I bring his face to mine.

Our lips meet and I can feel his hesitancy for a moment, before he relaxes and wraps his arms around me. Clint turns his head sideways and I crack my eyes open slightly to see the three men walk past us, still scanning the lobby.

One of the men's eyes stop on us for the briefest moment before he continues to look around. He walks out the front door just as I feel Clint bend me backwards slightly.

"Oi!" I hear the angry hiss from somewhere behind me, and break the kiss off.

Griffin is standing in the doorway off the main reception desk. His face is a mixture of anger and shock.

Clint pushes away from me and I nearly fall over.

Straightening up, I pick up my knapsack that fell to the ground.

"The van's out back," Griffin says, indicating over his shoulder while narrowing his eyes at Clint.

I follow behind Clint, who's ears are flaming red, through the kitchen and out the back door to the rear of the hotel.

"Ms Jenson, it's a pleasure to see you again," Omar greets me as I climb into the van after Clint.

Griffin gets in behind me and slams the car door, causing Clint to jump in his seat.

"Oh good, June, you made it," the Professor says from the back seat looking completely at ease. His trousers are back on, thank goodness.

"Where should we go now?" Dr Cooke says, leaning forward beside the Professor with a worried expression. "Should we find another hotel?"

"We will go to the British Embassy," the Professor says, matter-of-factly. "They'll know how to make a proper cup of tea there for certain."

Dr Cooke nods in agreement at the suggestion.

"Actually, I think we need to go to the Nile River," I say.

"June dear, I'm not sure any of us are up for sight seeing," Dr Cooke says, looking utterly exhausted.

"It's not for sight seeing," I say, and remembering that Omar can hear everything I say I lower my voice. "We've had a... *development.*"

"I'd say," Griffin says from beside me, still glaring at

JUNE JENSON AND THE KING'S LOST TREASURE

Clint. "Don't think I didn't see you trying to cop a feel."

"I did not!" Clint says, his face now scarlet to match his ears.

"Oh, don't be ridiculous," I say to Griffin. "I kissed him, anyways."

"What?" Griffin shouts, and I feel Clint flinch beside me.

"They were coming right for us, I had to do something so they wouldn't see our faces or think anything of us hiding behind the tree," I explain. "They weren't likely to think we'd be snogging while being chased."

"I—" he starts, but then seems lost for words.

"You snogged Clive?" the Professor asks, a disgusted look on his face.

"Alright, I'm not that bad!" Clint says, sitting straighter in his seat.

"Don't listen to them, you were fine," I say to him, patting his knee. "If not a little eager."

Clint looks a mixture of relieved and embarrassed.

"What about the Nile River?" Dr Cooke interjects. "Why would we need to go there?"

I look to Omar again, and my eyes meets his in the mirror for a split second before he quickly looks ahead. I turn more in my seat and lower my voice.

"Clint was unhooking the video camera before we left the room, and just as he was about to disconnect it I noticed something engraved on the boat on the petroglyph.

My eye was drawn to it, and I couldn't figure it out—but then I *saw* it. My brain must have seen it all along and I just never registered it with everything going on," I say, shaking my head.

I'm actually a bit disappointed in myself, if I'm being honest. I've always thought of my mind as my strongest asset.

"Saw what?" Dr Cooke asks, leaning forward in his seat.

"The hieroglyphic—the one from Quinn's paper," I say, widening my eyes and tilting my head in Omar's direction, trying to tell them not to say too much in the car.

"The boat said 'up' on it?" the Professor frowns.

Honestly, did he not see me gesturing to Omar?

"Yes," I say through gritted teeth. "But ex-nay on the up-ay."

I more forcefully gesture my head in Omar's direction.

"Why are you doing that with your head?" the Professor asks. "Is there a fly in here?"

"Oh God, is it a midge?" Dr Cooke quickly takes off his hat and starts waving it around at an imaginary mosquito. "They carry disease you know!"

"Oh, just forget it," I say, waving my hand.

"That's a bit of a stretch," Griffin says, shaking his head. "You don't really think that engraving means anything, do you?"

"Well, it's a pretty big coincidence," I point out.

"June, it was a boat going *up* stream," Griffin argues. "That's all that meant. Why for the love of God would they hide some clue to some lost treasure on a bloody piece of stone no one was ever likely to find?"

"Why don't you just shout from the roof tops what we're after," I angrily whisper.

"June, dear, it is a little... far fetched, you have to admit," Dr Cooke says.

"Is it, though?" I ask. "Ahmed Gamal donated that petroglyph. It said he had other items as well relating to the Tanis Pharaohs, but that was the piece he donated to the museum. What if he found all of the clues to get the ring, but then he lost the first clue thanks to our slippery friend, Mr. Quinn?"

"Yes, but why would he have donated one of the other clues?" Griffin asks.

"He has multiple artefacts from the Tanis Pharaohs—they are not all bound to be clues. Maybe he didn't know the petroglyph was a clue. He wouldn't have recognized the symbol on the boat because he can't remember what the hieroglyphic on the piece of paper was," I explain.

"I don't know," Griffin says, shaking his head. "The Nile River, that's pretty long isn't it?"

"Nearly seven thousand kilometres," Dr Cooke says, rubbing his jaw as he thinks.

"How the hell are we supposed to find a clue by travelling up seven thousand kilometres of water?" Clint asks, horrified. "I don't have enough room on my camera to film all that."

"I don't think we will have to travel up the whole thing," I say. I can see the Professor studying me from the corner of my eye.

"It would be in Thebes," the Professor says, nodding to my unasked question. "Surely, that's where the next clue would be."

"That's what I thought," I nod in agreement.

"Er—and why do we think that?" Griffin asks.

"Because that's where King Solomon lost it," the Professor answers.

"The ring?" Griffin asks, looking between the Professor and myself. "If you knew the ring was lost there this whole time, what have we been doing in Cairo?"

"Not the ring, boy," the Professor says. "His kingdom."

Chapter Nine

"I'm taking every last one, you bloody wench. Now, I didn't call you for a lecture—has the filter for the humidifier arrived? I need you to send it to me; my throat is closing up as we speak," the Professor yelps into the phone, futilely swatting away the thick air around him.

The noise from the busy marketplace seems to make the humidity in the air intolerable. The mix of spices in the air, the constant flow of people walking past, and the shouting from the different vendors trying to get customers into their makeshift shops is all a bit overwhelming. The throbbing in my temples indicates the migraine that is fast approaching. I shift my weight from one foot to the other, praying we will be on our way soon.

It's very unnerving being out in public with this many people around. The faces are becoming one big blur; my tired mind can't seem to keep up with processing all of their different features. My brain wants to lock them into my memory, but with the oncoming migraine, I can't seem to focus on anything as I stand here drenched in my own sweat.

Griffin's voice jolts me out of my thoughts.

"Everything is fine, Mum. No need to worry; they'll have us out of here in no time. It was just a little bomb scare." Griffin holds the phone away from his ear. I recognize Ruth's high-pitched screech.

"No, that's the box for the new sheets I had Clarence order. Bloody marvellous thing that internet—you never have to go to the shops again," the Professor says into the receiver in the telephone booth beside the one Griffin is standing in.

Dr Cooke pulls on the Professor's sleeve; they have wedged themselves into the cramped box together. The Plexiglas now completely fogged from the heat of their two bodies in the small space.

"Yes, alright," the Professor nods at him. "Daniel wants to know if a large box has arrived for him, as well."

"It's the defibrillator I ordered," Dr Cooke tries to yell into the receiver. "I want my own, if we both go at the same time I just *know* I would get the second round of shocks."

"How's she bloody meant to revive us both at the same time?" the Professor argues. "She'll have to do me first— you have life insurance."

"What's that bloody got to do with it?" Dr Cooke yells, trying to grab the phone out of the Professor's hand.

"Well if I go, you'll have nothing to enjoy. If you go, you can take comfort in the fact I will be sailing around the world on the insurance money," the Professor says, holding the phone out of Dr Cooke's reach.

"The cheek! I've left it to the bloody American Rock and Roll Hall of Fame just to piss you off!" Dr Cooke says, squeezing his body out of the booth and coming to stand beside me in a huff.

The sleeves of his shirt rolled up to his elbows, Dr Cooke stands next to me studying the marketplace in front of us, though I know he isn't really seeing any of it.

"Did you really?" I smile at him.

"I bloody should." Dr Cooke mutters, straightening his waistcoat.

"I'd pay to be in the room when they read out the will," I laugh, and after a moment a wide smile spreads across his face.

"Right, Omar thinks he's found someone," Clint comes to stand beside me, his shirt plastered to his thin frame with sweat. "He's just checking on the boat now to see if it will be suitable."

"Oh good," I say, fanning myself with a small brochure for a guided tour of the pyramids I was handed when we entered the market.

"The air is just stifling," Dr Cooke says, using his hat to fan himself. "I can barely breathe."

"We should be on the water soon; that will cool you down," I say, looking around for a sign of Omar. "It's nearly dusk, so we will need to leave soon."

"I'm not sure how much we will be able to see in the

dark, my dear," Dr Cooke says, turning his gaze to me. "The riverbanks are not likely to be lit."

"I know, but it's worth a shot. It just seems too dangerous right now to go on a tour in broad daylight with so many other people," I say. "I hate even standing here. I feel like someone is watching us."

My eyes dart around, but there is no one looking at us. I'm probably just being paranoid, and in this heat I feel like the rational part of my brain is slowly drifting away as I become more dehydrated.

"Well, you better get the two of them off the phone then and we'll go and try and find our trusty guide," Dr Cooke suggests.

I look back to the telephone booth, and Griffin hangs up the receiver and walks out towards us. He rolls his eyes in my direction, showing me his exasperation at his mother, and I smile again.

I look to the next phone booth, but it is empty.

"Where is the Professor?" I ask, turning my body around in a complete circle.

The different vendors have their arms raised, constantly shouting and beckoning tourists to come and look at their collection of goods for sale. With the end of the day nearing, people are walking in all different directions, some still entering the market but most trying to weave their way out of the crowds.

"He was just there," Dr Cooke says, frowning at the

empty booth.

"Did you see him leave?" I ask Griffin.

My eyes continue to scan through the throngs of people, but it is hard to focus on the ever-moving figures.

"No, he must have left when I had my back turned," Griffin frowns, his eyes also scanning the many faces that surround us. "We'll have to fan out and find him. He could be anywhere."

"Oh God," I say. I experience a sense of panic which I am sure if the same feeling parents get when they lose a small child in a busy crowd. *Where could he be?*

"Dr Cooke, you and Clint go up that way," Griffin points to the far aisle on our right. "June and I will go up this one, and we can both come down the centre to meet back here."

"We'll find him, June," Dr Cooke assures me, and quickly follows after Clint.

"Griffin, he could get in so much trouble here," I breathe out, the sense of panic heightened by the thick air around me.

"Come on," Griffin says, taking my hand.

We take a few steps up the farthest aisle to the left and stop as a man steps in front of us to block our path.

"Pretty shoes for the lady?" he asks, holding up a pair of purple flat-heeled shoes with jewels sewn onto them.

"Er—no thank you," I say, offering him a quick smile. We take a step to the side, but the man follows.

"What about some spices?" he says, trying to pull us into his hut.

"No, we are fine, thank you," Griffin says, pulling me further away from the shop.

"We have very pretty bangles," he yells after us but we quicken our pace, weaving through curious shoppers.

"Miss!" a young woman yells to me from up ahead. "Come and see my shop, please."

"The Professor wasn't bound to get far with all of this going on," Griffin says, keeping a vice like grip on my hand. "Don't make eye contact with them, they will get the message."

But they don't. As we continue to make our way to the top of the market we are stopped an additional three times, and practically dragged into make-shift shops.

"No, we are not interested," Griffin holds up his hand before the next person even speaks. "We are looking for someone."

He doesn't wait for a response and I almost fall over at the force at which he is dragging me through the crowd.

"Griffin, can you please slow down? I'm going to trip!" I say, and I bump into someone stopped in the middle of the aisle, gazing at some paintings of the pyramids displayed on the wall outside a hut.

"I hate shopping," Griffin says in exasperation. "Mum used to drag me to all those bloody car boot sales, drove me up the wall—and she never bought a bloody thing."

I smile to myself as we turn the corner and start walking down the next aisle.

My eye catches something and I stop. I yank Griffin's arm to get him to stop pulling me along.

"What is it? Is it the Professor?" Griffin asks, scanning the crowd in front of him.

"No," I shake my head.

I pull him to the side so we are half hidden by the wall of the closest hut, though my eyes never leave the sight in front of me.

"What is it?" Griffin repeats.

"Look!" I say, and try to subtly point in the direction I am looking, making sure to keep my voice down.

"Where?" Griffin asks.

"By that shop that has the statues," I say, nodding my head in the general direction.

I look at Griffin as his eyes search, and I can tell instantly when he sees it.

He frowns.

"What the hell—" he mutters. "What are they doing together?"

I turn my eyes back to where Griffin is looking.

Thomas is standing in the shadows of a small hut that has sphinx statues on display, stacked on tables just peeking out past the shop walls. I watch as he takes out a small notepad and starts to write down something   The dishevelled figure of Quinn stands next to him, nervously shaking his head.

"He doesn't want Thomas writing down what he is saying," I guess, tilting my head towards Griffin so he can hear me.

"What could the two of them possibly be talking about?" Griffin asks.

"He's probably selling him a clue to some other long lost artefact," I say, shaking my head.

"Or the same clue as he sold us," Griffin says in disgust.

I shake my head.

"No, I would swear the paper clue we have is original. Unless he copied the symbol and is just selling that," I amend.

The thought makes my already warm body seethe with rage. Not because we potentially got swindled. I think the moment I laid eyes on Quinn I knew there was a very fair likelihood of that happening. No, it's the fact that he is telling anyone and everyone how to find the ring that bothers me. He doesn't care what they will do with it, or what they want it for. I know I shouldn't really expect any less from a man like him, but it makes the urgency to find the ring that much greater.

Thomas flips the page in his notebook to show Quinn something, but it seems like that's the final straw. Quinn shakes his head more forcefully, puts his hands up, and walks away from Thomas—right in our direction.

Thomas follows after him and Griffin and I both turn our heads quickly so our faces are not visible to those walking by. After a moment I look up in the direction we just came from to see Quinn turning the corner, Thomas still following after him.

"Come on," Griffin says, taking my hand again. "We need to find the Professor and the others and get out of here."

"You don't think he is renting a boat as well, do you?" I ask Griffin's back as I follow him once again through the crowd. "Do you think he knows what the clue means?"

"I don't know," Griffin says over his shoulder. "But it didn't really look like Quinn was exactly cooperating, so let's hope not."

Still not a single sign of the Professor.

"We don't need any rugs!" Griffin holds his hand up to one man who has now followed us five shops down, all while trying to unroll a massive red rug and walk at the same time.

"We offer free shipping," the man says, running his hand over the weaving.

"No, really, we—" Griffin stops what he is saying at the sight of Dr Cooke hurrying up the aisle towards us.

"Oh thank God! Do you have any money?" he yells, panting but still racing in our direction.

"What? What's happened?" I ask.

But he doesn't need to explain. I look up to see the

Professor coming along quickly behind him, followed closely by Clint.

I look at the Professor, who has a bottle in each hand and frown.

"What the bloody—" Griffin starts.

Dr Cooke finally makes it to us and darts behind us, using us as a shield.

The Professor has changed his clothes, now wearing a loose fitting cream coloured tunic shirt that falls down to his ankles.

"He's after me! He's after me!" the Professor says, taking a swig from one bottle and turning to the other before he's even had a chance to swallow the first mouth full.

"What is that? Where are your trousers?" I ask him, looking down at his sandal clad feet.

The Professor stops in front of me, swaying slightly. His blue eyes are unfocused behind his rimless glasses, and he blinks rapidly as he tries to place me.

"This is a traditional Egyptian garment called a Galabia. It does wonders for keeping the body cool in this heat. I traded a bloke my trousers for them," the Professor hiccups, bringing one of the bottles to his lips again.

Clint stands behind him, his hand clutching his side; he is keeled over and panting heavily.

"You—didn't—no—money," Clint tries to get out between deep gasps.

"What? What's going on?" I ask, but am once again distracted by another man, wearing a tunic like the Professor's, running up the aisle and shaking his fist and yelling Arabic words.

"What have you done?" I hiss at the Professor as the angry man finally makes it to where we are huddled.

"You give me no money!" he yells at the Professor, taking one of the bottles out of his unresisting hand.

"Calm down, I don't have any," the Professor says, waving away the concern and sending himself off balance. He stumbles slightly but manages to stay on his feet "My assistant here will pay you. He's got heaps of money in his bag."

The Professor nods to Clint and winks.

Clint looks at the Professor as though he is about to throttle him.

"I do not!" Clint says, and quickly brings the bag up to his chest.

I look around the market and see everyone in the vicinity has stopped to watch our exchange. Some of the nearby shop owners are now eyeing Clint's bag with interest.

"I don't," Clint says, more to the growing crowd now, shaking his head.

"What happened to all of that money you were throwing about at the American's house?" the Professor asks, slurring his words.

Clint's face flushes.

"Professor," I hiss. "Be quiet!"

"Give me the bottle, you bloody fool," Dr Cooke says, snatching the remaining bottle from the Professor. "You could never hold your liquor."

The man who came running after the Professor taps Clint on the shoulder and he jumps from the contact.

"You have money, so you pay me now!" the man demands.

"I don't," Clint turns his imploring gaze to me.

"How much does he owe you?" I intervene.

"For the wine and the garment: three thousand pounds," the man states.

"Three thousand! Is it spun with bloody gold?" Griffin asks in outrage, and I put my hand on his arm to calm him down.

"He means Egyptian pounds, not British," I explain, and then turn my attention back to the man. "I'm sorry we do not have that. We will pay for the wine, but we'll have to give you the garment back. If you could just return my grandfather's trousers…"

"I do not have his trousers!" the man says, looking to the Professor. "I sell, I do not trade."

I sigh in exasperation.

"Where are you trousers?" I ask the Professor, who is now studying some spices outside of the closest shop. I have no idea what he thinks he is currently looking at, but he squints his eyes in an attempt to read the labels.

"Er—" he says, looking around in search of them.

I close my eyes for a moment to gain patience.

"How much money do you have on you?" I turn to ask Griffin.

"About twenty quid," Griffin says, feeling inside his pocket. "What's the conversion rate?"

"It's roughly one hundred and twenty pounds," I say, shaking my head in frustration.

Griffin swears under his breath

"Clint, do you have anything?" I ask, trying to keep my voice as low as possible.

"Just the money for the boat," Clint shakes his head. "Omar says we will need all of it."

"Dr Cooke?" I ask turning around.

"Nothing, I'm afraid my dear," he says.

I turn to Griffin.

"His extra clothes are in the car. I could go back and get a pair of his trousers. I have some spare money at the bottom of my cosmetics case I think."

"It will take you half an hour to get there and back if you're lucky," Griffin argues. "We will miss the boat."

"Well, we can't stand in the middle of the market here. We don't want to *bump* into anyone," I say to Griffin, widening my eyes.

The man watches our exchange, before tapping me on the shoulder.

"I accept Visa," he says.

Chapter Ten

"I don't like this," Griffin says, holding onto the railing of the boat as we rock back and forth.

"What *do* you like?" I ask, trying not to let my exasperation show.

Honestly. It's not like I'm having the time of my life here. I'm not particularly fond of boats. I don't like the way they move. And I'm not particularly thrilled with bodies of water since I nearly died in that well last year. I'm currently trying to keep my eyes on the shore to stop from being sick, but he doesn't hear *me* complaining.

Mainly because he hasn't shut up enough to give me the chance.

"Anything *but* this," he says, shaking his head while nervously looking up and down the shoreline.

"Where's your sense of adventure?" I ask. "It's actually quite beautiful out here, under Egypt's night sky with all of the stars. Not a building in sight, just the glow of the moon."

I stand next to Griffin and rest my head on his shoulder.

"Hmm... you're sure you wouldn't rather be out under

the night sky with Clint?" he asks.

"Nope," I say, lifting my face to smile at him. "I've already kissed *him* today."

Griffin smiles slightly, looking down at my face.

"Tired of him already, are you?" he asks

I grin and nod.

"Good," he says, and brings his lips to mine.

"June, there you are!" the Professor yells from behind me, causing Griffin and I to break apart.

The boat is only forty feet long, with a single deck. The gleaming wooden floors shine in the moonlight, making it almost impossible not to see every square inch of boat's deck and all its occupants. Though I haven't seen much of the Captain and Omar—they are huddled together by the ship's controls at the front of the boat.

"I've just been having a bit of a word with our Captain, and as it so happens he is single and looking for a special someone in his life," the Professor winks.

Oh good Lord, not again.

"Now, I explained that you are just shy of forty, but it didn't really seem to bother him too much."

"I'll be forty in three years!" I say as the heat rises to my cheeks. "That's hardly shy of anything."

"That's what you have a problem with?" Griffin asks, his one eyebrow raised.

"Er—no, sorry, you're right. Professor, please, I'm fine," I say, and feel Griffin's stare on my flushed face.

"You do not need to find me a husband. Perhaps write that in your journal."

The Professor's smile is unflinching and I realize he's not quite with us right now.

"Albert, there you are," Dr Cooke comes to stand beside the Professor. "One minute you have me looking at the propellers and the next thing I know you're gone."

"The Professor has been match-making for June again," Griffin says, trying to convey the Professor's current state to Dr Cooke.

"Have you two been talking marriage?" Dr Cooke's face lights up as he looks between Griffin and myself. "Oh June, I'm so pleased for you. I know how much you've been wanting this."

"I have not!" I say instinctively, and if possible my face gets even warmer. "I said no such thing."

"The Professor has been talking to the boat captain," Griffin explains, though never takes his eyes off me.

"Oh dear," Dr Cooke purses his lips.

"Perhaps you could take the Professor back to the port side?" I ask Dr Cooke. "I'm worried we might miss something if we don't have both sides covered."

Dr Cooke looks from Griffin's studying gaze to my twitching smile.

"Yes, of course," Dr Cooke says, taking the Professor's arm. "Come with me, Albert."

"Was it something I said?" he tilts his head at Dr

Cooke.

"Er—yes. That always seems to be the case, doesn't it?" Dr Cooke laughs.

I turn back to look at the dark shoreline, carefully avoiding Griffin's gaze.

"So what was all that about, then?" Griffin quietly asks.

"Oh, you know the Professor," I force a laugh. "Don't pay him any attention."

Griffin says nothing for a moment, and I shift uncomfortably to the other foot.

"You know, I always thought you didn't really want to get married," Griffin says, putting his hands out to rest on the top rail.

"Griffin, please don't let what the Professor said put ideas in your head," I force a casual laugh. "You know what he's like."

"Oh, I know," Griffin says, running his hand through his tousled hair. "And you said yourself in the museum that you didn't want to get married, right?"

"Well, actually, I said I didn't *have* to get married," I say, resting my arms on the railing

"Okay..." Griffin nods. "So that's not the same thing?"

"I said I don't *have* to get married. Not that I don't *want* to get married," I argue.

"What's the difference?" he asks.

"The difference is that I don't *have* to get married to

have a fulfilling life," I say.

"But you *want* to get married to have a fulfilling life?" he asks.

I throw my hands up in the air.

"I don't *have* to eat chocolate cake, but it doesn't mean that I might not *want* a slice of it every once and a while," I say, standing up straight and wiping my hands down the front of my trousers.

I'm not quite sure why I am getting riled up about this. I mean, the whole thing is just ridiculous.

"So you sometimes want to get married?" he asks, rubbing his jaw.

"No—I—I didn't say that," I say, shaking my head.

"So, you don't *have* to get married, and you don't *want* to get married..." Griffin pauses. "So, how is it not the same thing?"

Well, he's just completely missed the bloody point.

"It—it just isn't," I say, shaking my head. "Can we please just forget about it?"

"Found anything yet?" the Professor asks, coming to stand beside me once more with Dr Cooke.

"Well, we were nearly on to something there," Griffin says, giving me a pointed look.

"Nothing on our side," Dr Cooke says, gesturing to the other end of the boat. "Though it's next to impossible to see anything in the dark."

"Can't tell our arse from our elbow," the Professor

says, shaking his head.

"We had to hire the boat at night time," I explain for the tenth time, thankful for the change in subject. "The regular tour boats don't come so close to the shore. It was very lucky that Omar convinced this man to take us out at all."

"Well, it was a waste of money, if you ask me," Dr Cooke says, wiping his forehead with his handkerchief. "Does it never get cool in this God forsaken country?"

"Clifford's nearly used up all the space on his camera," the Professor says.

I look behind him to see Clint filming from the other side of the boat, the little red light from his camera shining bright through the dark.

"Good, I'll be able to watch it back in case we've missed anything," I say.

Clint makes his way over to us, the camera still turned on and now pointing in the direction we are all staring in.

"If there is anything to be missed, we surely have," Dr Cooke says, shaking his head. "It's no good June, we can't see anything in this light."

"Yes, and we are nearly at the end of Thebes anyways," I sigh. "We will have to try again during the day and bring binoculars."

"Maybe you got the location wrong," Griffin suggests. "It's a needle in a haystack. There might not even be a clue; or we might not be looking in the right place for it."

"It would be in Thebes—I'm sure of it," I say, scanning the shoreline again.

"How can you be so sure?" Griffin asks.

"Because, during the end of King Solomon's reign there began a civil war in Egypt. Remember, King Solomon had lost God's favour due to his wandering eye, and God brought unrest to his kingdom because of it. There was an invasion, and during the war the supplies to Thebes were cut off because they were unable to get past the army up river on the Nile," I say, pointing to the vast water in front of us. "Grain shipments were delivered along the Nile river and without access the people began to suffer."

"What does that have to do with the ring?" Griffin asks.

"By the time the real hardship had set it, King Solomon had died—or the Tanis Pharaoh died, if you believe they were one in the same," I explain. "He was buried in the Valley of the Kings on the West Bank of Thebes."

I point to the left of the boat.

"Without the King, and the people starving, there were plunderings all over the land for the vast treasures that Solomon had accumulated," I say.

"I must be missing something," Griffin shakes his head. "If people plundered the graves, then someone surely would have taken the ring."

"Yes, unless someone took it to protect it before they

could," I say.

"What are you talking about?" Clint interjects, the camera now trained on my face.

"The Holy Grail was moved by the Knights Templar to stop thieves for getting it," I explain. "Why can it not be concluded then, that someone took the ring for the exact same reason? Because they didn't want the opposing army, or some thief who would melt it down for gold, to have it."

"But there is absolutely no proof that anyone did do that," Griffin argues.

"Of course there is," I say, shaking my head. "It's what we are looking for, isn't it? Someone took the ring from King Solomon's tomb before the grave robbers could get there, and left clues like the piece of paper—just like the Knight's Templar did for the Grail—for those worthy enough to find it."

"I—Do you two believe this?" Griffin asks, turning to the Professor and Dr Cooke.

Dr Cooke purses his lips while the Professor looks at me thoughtfully.

"The marking was on the petroglyph," the Professor says.

"It is possible," Dr Cooke concedes.

"Possible, but not likely," Griffin says.

"My boy, the search for history is founded on much less than possible," the Professor says, leaning against the rail and peering over the edge. "June, there's something shiny down there!"

It happens in the blink of an eye. The Professor leans far over the rail, and then his legs are up over his head and there's a loud splash.

"Oh good Lord!" I say, running over the edge of the deck. "Stop the boat!"

The Captain peeks his head out from his little hut at the front of the boat.

"What was that, miss?" he yells to me.

"Stop the boat! Man overboard!" I yell back, and he nods.

I feel the lurch of the boat beneath my feet as the engine is cut.

The Professor's head bops up from under the water and he sputters.

"I can't swim!" he screams, flailing his arms. "I can't swim!"

"Yes you can! You know how, just kick out your legs!" I yell at him. "Try and get over to the side of the boat, and we can pull you back up. It's only a four foot drop."

"My hat!" the Professor says in panic as his mustard coloured hat starts floating away from him. "The Prime Minister gave me that hat!"

"You bought it from Asda, you bloody idiot!" Dr Cooke yells down to him as we all lean over the rail.

"I'll have to go in and get him," I say, taking off my backpack.

"You can't go in there!" Griffin says. "I thought you were afraid of water ever since Colorado."

My eyes widen momentarily as I remember my time trapped at the bottom of the well in Colorado. I fell down into it while we were searching for Butch Cassidy's treasure and broke my leg. I would have drowned if it weren't for Griffin diving in and pulling me out.

"Well, I can't let him drown," I say, pointing over the side of the boat.

Besides, they say you are supposed to face your fears to overcome them, don't they? I can't see a better way of testing that theory than jumping into the Nile in the middle of the night, with God knows what lurking beneath the water.

"I'll go and get him," Griffin says, kicking off his shoes.

"No, it's alright. I can do it," I say to him, taking off my own shoes.

"I'm not going to let you jump into the Nile in the middle of the bloody night when you're afraid of the water, am I?" Griffin asks, pulling his shirt up and over his head.

"Griffin, I am more than capable—"

"Would one of you get in this ruddy water and save me before I *drown*!" the Professor splutters from below.

"Every bloody time something happens..." Griffin mutters, before climbing up on the rail and jumping into the water.

"Alright, get a hold of him, and we'll pull him back up!"

I say when Griffin comes up above water.

"You can touch the ground!" Griffin says, in exasperation as he wades over to the Professor, the water just below his neck.

"Did you feel that?" the Professor says, his eyes widening. "Was that an eel?"

"If there are bloody eels in here, I'm leaving you!" Griffin says, and starts to scan the pitch black water.

"Get over here!" I say to both of them.

Griffin grabs the Professor after unceremoniously jamming his hat back on his head and then wades over to the boat.

"Right, now give him a bit of a boost," I say when they are finally at the edge of the boat.

"And how would you suggest I do that?" Griffin asks.

Both he and the Professor look up at the three of us, leaning over the rail of the boat, their heads the only thing visible over the water's surface.

"You know, just, grab him around the middle…" I say, my arms making a big circle in front of me, showing Griffin what to do. "And, lift him up."

They both stare at me, then look to each other.

"Well, you heard her," the Professor says to Griffin.

I hear Griffin mutter something under his breath, but can't hear the exact words. Though, I'm not sure you'd have to be a rocket scientist to figure out what they are.

"Right, on three!" Griffin says, standing behind the

Professor. "One, two, three!"

The Professor's torso emerges from the water.

"Grab him!" Griffin splutters through a mouth full of water.

Which is easier said than done. The Professor's arms are waving every which way.

"Stay still!" Clint yells, trying to grab one of the Professor's arms.

"It's like holding on to a flailing octopus!" Dr Cooke says, finally managing to hold onto one of the Professor's hands.

"Right," I say, when Clint finally has the other one. "Now pull him up!"

"I've got you, Albert!" Dr Cooke says, giving a massive tug and then leaning back over the railing.

"He's so slippery!" Clint yells, and I see his feet leave the ground as he tries to hold onto the Professor's arm.

"Ah!" Dr Cooke yells, and before I can do anything to stop them, they are both over the railing and into the water, falling on top of the Professor and Griffin.

"Oh good God!" I yell, leaning over the rail.

"What's happened?" The Captain comes running over to me and together we lean over the railing.

"Another three men overboard," I say, pointing down to the water.

"I'm drowning! I'm drowning!" Dr Cooke splutters as he comes to the surface.

"Put your feet down!" Griffin and I both yell at the same time.

"Oh, yes, right," he says, but because of his height, only his nose and forehead are above the water.

"We will have to pull the boat onto the bank," the Captain says, looking down at the four men in the water, an amused look on his face.

"Okay," I agree.

"I'll go start the motor again and turn us to the West Bank," he says, stepping away from the railing.

"Right! You lot wade your way over to the shore, we're bringing the boat around!" I yell down to them.

I hear them all grumble, but their floating heads turn and start to drift towards the shore. I'm not sure whether the sight of it is comical or eerie.

Honestly, I just don't know if the night could get any worse.

We've found nothing. We have nothing.

I don't know if Simon will accept my theory, because quite frankly we have nothing to back it up with. And, if he doesn't accept it—well, I'm not really sure where that leaves us.

But, if I'm being honest, that's not *really* what's bothering me. What's bothering me is that I know that I am on to something. I realize I don't have a lot of facts to back it up and its ninety-five percent just a hunch… But, I know I am right.

But how am I going to prove it? How am I going to see this thing through?

It is so dangerous here—and not just because we are in the middle of a war-torn country. Because there is *that*.

No, it's more the Egyptian mob that is my immediate concern right now.

I just know, though, that if I had the luxury of time and didn't have to avoid my imminent capture and death, I could most definitely solve this puzzle.

My body gets thrown into the side of the railing as the boat suddenly stops again.

"This is as close as I can get, because there is no dock," the Captain yells to me from the front. "Your guide is putting down the anchor. There's a ladder on the port side, the water won't be too deep. You can wade to the shore and get your friends. We shall wait on the boat for you."

"Right," I say, looking down at my white trousers. "Well, this should be interesting."

I walk over to where the Captain pointed and look over the rail at the flimsy rope ladder hanging down.

"That doesn't look too sturdy," I say, eyeing the frayed rope warily.

"Oh, she'll hold," the Captain says, nodding reassuringly.

"Hmm…"

Not entirely convinced, I throw my leg over the railing and try to get my foot situated on the top rung of the ladder.

"How close are we to the top of Thebes anyways?" I ask.

"You're looking at it," the Captain says, pointing behind me. "There's the sign for the two paths away from Thebes."

"We travelled the whole Western Bank?" I ask, pulling my other leg over the railing so both feet are firmly on the ladder.

The captain nods.

"When your friends are back on board we will need to head back," he says.

"Of course," I say.

"June!" I hear from behind me, and turn my head to see the Professor running along the river bank towards the boat, wearing only his underpants. "June, I'm alive!"

Griffin, Dr Cooke, and Clint walk behind the Professor, none of them looking very pleased. Especially Griffin, who appears to be carrying the Professor's clothes.

"Wonderful!" I yell back before turning my head the other way to scan the Eastern Bank in the distance, but it is too far and too dark to see much of it.

I wonder for a moment whether we should travel along the Eastern Bank on our way back, but then quickly dismiss it.

No, the Valley of the Kings is on the Western Bank. His tomb is on the Western Bank. The clue would most certainly be on the Western Bank.

But we didn't see it, I remind myself.

But it has to be there. It is dark, that's why we didn't see it. We will have to come back during the day. Of course, it won't be as safe as we won't be alone, and we will be on a much larger tour boat so we won't be able to get as close to the shore as we are in this smaller boat. But it's the only option we have now.

My eyes travel back to the bank where the Professor is running, but stops suddenly on the marked sign in the middle of the split in the river.

It's an old sign, made of stone, not dissimilar in size to the petroglyph sitting on the ground amongst the trees. From fifty yards away it would be impossible to even know it was there if it weren't for the boat's front lights shining on the particular spot.

The Captain comes to stand by the railing and we both squint at the sign.

"It is quite remarkable, isn't it?" he asks, nodding in the direction of the land. "We are very proud of our culture and history in Egypt. Our people take a lot of care to preserve things that are centuries old."

"I'm surprised you can see it in the dark," I say to him, squinting to try and see it better. "I would have missed it completely."

"Most of us who sail the Nile know it like the back of our hands," the Captain says, shrugging. "Also, the tourists like these ancient signs."

"Well, I suppose you can see the fork in the river even if you miss the sign," I say, still squinting and taking one of my hands off the railing to push my glasses further up nose. "What is that writing on it?"

"It is giving the two directions of the river," the Captain explains.

"To Luxor?" I ask.

"They weren't quite that specific in ancient times," the Captain says, laughing. "The local Egyptians didn't abide by North and South during those times when traveling on the Nile. The top inscription says 'up', and the bottom inscription says 'down'."

I hear his words, but they are drowned out by the sudden buzzing noise in my ears, and the view seems to fade away.

The top says 'up' and the bottom says 'down'.

And suddenly I forget to hold onto the ladder.

I hit the water, my bum hitting the hard sandy floor, causing the wind to be knocked out of me. I feel the water engulfing my face and I freeze, unable to move.

I know I *can* move, but at the same time, I am unable to move. I am paralyzed and feel frozen in time. I'm not here, not in Egypt. No, suddenly I am thousands of miles away, in a well in a forest in Colorado and water is quickly filling up around me. I can't move because my legs refuse to budge. I want to move, to kick up and bring my head above the water, but no matter how much my brain screams for my body to take action, I'm frozen in place and can't seem to get my limbs to listen.

Suddenly a strong arm wraps around my waist and I gasp for air as my head breaks the surface of the water.

"June, put your feet down!" Griffin yells, and it takes a moment for me to realize he's pulled me up out of the water. Again.

"I—I just got the wind knocked out of me when I fell," I say to him, scrambling to put my shaking legs on the ground and put my weight on them.

I finally manage to right myself and I can feel Griffin's gaze inspecting me.

"You're sure you're alright?" he says, his concern evident.

I smooth back the wet hair from my face and push my glasses back into place, thankful I didn't lose them in the dark water.

"I'm fine," I say, reaching out my wet hand to touch his cheek. "We really need to stop making this a habit."

I offer him a smile, but I can tell he is too concerned to find the humour in the situation at the moment.

"Did you slip?" he asks, looking from the rope ladder back to me.

"No, I let go," I say, frowning. "I—"

"June, we saw the fall," the Professor says, now standing next to us, out of breath and up to his waist in water. His pale skin almost translucent under the Egyptian stars. "Very ungraceful."

"Thank you for your concern," I say, rolling my eyes.

"Did you get bit by something?" Dr Cooke asks, swatting an imaginary fly from around his face. "Bloody midges are everywhere!"

"No, I... I let go by accident, I—" I look at them, still unable to comprehend it. "I found the clue."

"You did?" Dr Cooke asks, his wide eyes quickly scanning the bank. "Where?"

"There," I say, pointing behind them to the boulder.

"That rock?" Clint asks, squinting in it's direction.

"It's the directional sign for this section of the Nile River. The ancient people of Thebes inscribed it—the Captain told me." I gesture over my shoulder towards the boat.

"So, what's the clue?" Griffin says, squinting at the rock also.

"It says '*up*' on the top, in ancient hieroglyphics, and below it says the word '*down*'," I say, and frown when the others stare at me, unresponsive. "What?"

"That's not a bloody clue," the Professor says, shaking his head. "That's just a sign to give people directions."

"It has the word 'up' written *just* like the clue on the paper," I argue.

"Yes, but June, we're in Egypt," Dr Cooke says scratching his forehead. "There's bound to be the word 'up' written in hieroglyphics on a number of things all over this country, isn't there? There not all going to be the lost clue."

"Yes, but one of them will be," I say, putting my hands on my hips. "And this is the only thing on the West Bank of Thebes with that word engraved."

"That we've seen," Dr Cooke says. "It's pitch dark, we could have missed the clue miles ago."

"If there is a clue," Clint adds, wiping the water off his forehead. "This whole thing could be a wild goose chase."

"It's not," I say to him.

"Oh yeah, and how do you know that?" he asks, raising his eyebrows at my certainty.

"I just... I just know, I can't explain it," I say. "I have no proof, and I realize that sign could mean nothing. But for some reason, I know it means *something*."

"June, I don't know," Griffin says, rubbing the back of his neck. "I mean, the other stuff, that stone thing in the museum, that was all a little far-fetched. But this..."

"Griffin, I know this is it," I say, pointing at the boulder. "I just know, and I need you to trust me on this."

We stare at each other, and after a moment he sighs, raising his arms in defeat.

"If you say so..." he hedges.

"Well, I don't bloody say so!" the Professor says, wading his way over to the bottom rung of the ladder. "Up, down, it doesn't mean a bloody thing."

I sigh and look at Dr Cooke, who is studying me intently, and I see a note of pity on his face.

"You don't think it means anything, either?" I ask.

"June, you know I would follow you to the ends of the earth," Dr Cooke says, and slaps the side of his neck, killing an insect. "Well, my dear, we've reached it and unfortunately there is naff all here."

He walks past me, and follows the Professor up the ladder.

I turn to Clint and raise my eyebrows.

"Er—it's an interesting theory, for sure," Clint says, nodding his head. "I mean, it would make great television, wouldn't it?"

"But you agree with them?" I ask him, crossing my arms across my chest.

"Well… I mean…" Clint says, scratching the side of his head.

"Forget it," I say, throwing my arms up. "Just forget it. I know you all think I'm crazy."

"No one thinks you're crazy, June," Griffin says, reaching his hand out to touch my arm.

I turn away from it though, and wade over to the ladder.

I pull myself up and start climbing, but stop and turn one more time to look at the rock.

"Er—let's see if the Captain has some towels on board, shall we?" Griffin asks from the bottom of the ladder.

His voice breaks my concentration and I look down at him.

"It's like ninety degrees outside, we will be dry in no time," I tell him.

"Oh, it's not that," he says, a smile tugging at his lips. "It's just... well, your trousers have turned completely see-through."

I look down at my white trousers and sigh.

Chapter Eleven

I sit in our new hotel room, drumming my fingers on the small table next to the kitchenette.

"Fancy a game of cards?" Griffin asks from across the room, his arms crossed as he stares at the wall.

"No thanks," I say, looking at my watch for what feels like the millionth time that hour.

"What about a little television?" Dr Cooke asks, to which he only receives grumbling as a reply.

"What about a drink?" the Professor suggests, and then sinks back into his chair at my disapproving stare.

"God, I'm bored!" Clint says, dropping his head onto the table next to me.

"Four days, it's been four ruddy days and that airport is still closed!" Dr Cooke says, shaking his head. "This would *never* happen in England."

"Of course it wouldn't happen in England," the Professor lashes out, waving his journal at Dr Cooke. "We all *know* it wouldn't happen in England, there's no sense in rubbing it in!"

"Oh, but it's fine when you have a moan, isn't it?" Dr

Cooke snaps back.

"I–" the Professor starts.

"Oh, give it a rest, the pair of you," Clint yells, his forehead still on the table. "You're both doing my bloody head in!"

We all turn to stare at him, but his head doesn't move.

The doorbell to the suite rings and I jump from my chair.

"I'll get it!" I say, rushing over.

"June, you best let me," Griffin says, getting up and hurrying over to me. "We weren't expecting anyone."

"Actually, I was," I say and staring back at me through the peephole is Omar.

I open the door and beckon him in.

"What's Omar here for?" the Professor asks, sitting up straighter. "Are we going out somewhere? Do they have alcohol there?"

I ignore the Professor and bring Omar over to the table, his arms laden with folders.

"Did you manage to get it all?" I ask him as he puts the pile down onto the table.

"Everything you asked for, Ms Jenson," Omar nods, and looks at the piles of paper.

I can tell he wants to ask what I am going to do with them, but I give nothing away.

"Will that be everything?" he finally asks.

"Yes, thank you," I say, leading him back to the door.

"If I need anything else, I will be sure to ring you. Oh, and Omar—thank you."

He nods once and leaves, closing the suite door behind him.

"What's this?" Dr Cooke says, getting up from the couch.

"Er—I've asked Omar to just get a few things for me from the library," I say, walking back over to the table where Clint is eyeing the papers suspiciously.

"What sort of things?" the Professor asks, coming to stand beside the table.

"Just a little background reading about Egypt," I say, shrugging, and begin to collect the papers off the table. "I don't want to bother anyone, so I'll just take them into my room—"

"I wouldn't mind a little reading," Dr Cooke says, taking one of the file folders out of my hand. "Might help pass the time."

"What has he brought?" the Professor says, peering over Dr Cooke's shoulder.

Dr Cooke looks at me in exasperation, before turning to look at the Professor.

"A full account of any artefacts relating to the Tanis Pharaoh's tomb," Dr Cooke says.

The Professor studies me for a moment and I raise my chin defiantly.

Honestly, just because they all gave up on it doesn't

mean I have to.

"Still fighting that battle are we, June Bug?" the Professor asks, slightly bemused.

"Always," I answer.

"Right, well I'll start with this one," the Professor says, taking another folder out of my arms.

"I thought you had both concluded this was all rubbish?" I say, raising my eyebrows.

"Oh, it most certainly is," the Professor says, taking off his glasses and cleaning them on his shirt. "But frankly I've pursued much more foolish things with considerably less time on my hands."

"I can vouch for that," Dr Cooke says, pulling out one of the chairs at the table.

"Right, and you?" I ask, turning to Griffin.

He eyes the piles of folders and forces a look of regret on his features.

"I think I might actually try a bit of writing," he says, stretching out his arms. "Because I think the old 'I don't have any time to write' won't fly now, will it?"

Griffin turns and disappears into our bedroom.

The chair next to me scrapes back, and Clint jumps to his feet.

"I think I will start editing some of the footage—see what I can put together," Clint says, quickly picking up his camera and going into his own bedroom.

"Right, just us three then," I say, taking a seat at the

table.

"And what needle are we trying to find in this haystack?" Dr Cooke asks, opening the folder in his hand.

"Well, Ahmed Gamal has rotated some of his pieces into the museum over the years, and some have been photographed at his home when he hosted different events there," I say, picking up another folder from the pile. "I wanted to look at them and read their documented descriptions to see if I could find the 'down' hieroglyphic on anything."

"If that was the next clue," the Professor reminds me.

"It's all I have to go on," I shrug.

And, also, I know I am right about it. It's the only thing that logically makes sense. And logic hasn't failed me yet.

Well, not a lot, anyways.

"He can't own all of these artefacts, surely," Dr Cooke says, flipping through all of the pages.

"No, I had Omar find the records for all of the artefacts that have been linked to the Pharaohs—however distant," I say. "Though, in all honesty, I'm sure Ahmed Gamal owns many artefacts we *don't* know about."

"And Omar didn't want to know why you wanted all of this?" Dr Cooke asks.

"He thinks we are here to do a story on the artefacts," I say, shrugging. "He just doesn't know the story is about one that hasn't been found yet."

"Right, so what exactly are we looking for?" the Professor says, spilling one of the file folder's contents all over the floor.

"Something with the word 'down' on it. It could be in hieroglyphics, or Hebrew, perhaps," I say.

No one says any more for ages. The only sounds are the rustling of pages and the Professor sighing after discarding each piece he looks at.

It's got to be here somewhere. It's just got to be.

"Well, this is interesting," Dr Cooke says, shifting in his chair.

"What is it?" I ask. I rise and quickly walk over to stand behind his chair, leaning over his shoulder to look.

"This wall that was unearthed on the Temple Mount," Dr Cooke says, showing me the picture in his hand. "It was unearthed less than a decade ago near Jerusalem."

"Does it have any markings on it?" I ask, squinting at the picture.

"No, but it does align with the biblical story of King Solomon building a defensive wall around the first temple. A temple which would have stored his most valuable treasures," Dr Cooke explains. "Perhaps Jerusalem would be a good place to search."

"Perhaps," I say, frowning. "But, we aren't really talking about a buried artefact, we are talking about a *hidden* one. Something somebody took to keep it safe. It will be in a very specific, meaningful place."

"If it exists," the Professor qualifies.

"If it exists," I agree.

"What about this," the Professor says, his spectacles sitting on the tip of his nose as he reads the paper in front of him. "A woman's remains were found only last year in Timna where it is rumoured Solomon's copper mines were."

He hands me the piece of paper and I quickly read it.

"They found a grave with her bones, and her unborn child," I say, looking up and frowning. "It's very unusual for them to find the remains of a woman with child where mining work would have been taking place. Why would she have been so far from home?"

"It is intriguing," the Professor pauses. "She wouldn't have been the wife of one of the workers—they would never have brought her there, and she certainly wouldn't have been permitted to stay. Women stayed in their villages while their husbands went away to work."

"It says only a part of her skeleton were found—only her lower half," I say, biting my lip in concentration. "That's very odd. It was buried in a grave. Why would only her bottom half be there?

"Looters?" Dr Cooke suggests.

"What would they want with the top half of her body?" I ask, frowning.

"It doesn't make sense," the Professor says, shaking his head. "She shouldn't be there in the first place—any part of her. The only people who would have been there are workers or someone of nobility, someone that was Solomon's guest."

"You don't suppose..." I pause, and then shake my head in dismissal.

"What?" Dr Cooke asks.

"Well, you don't suppose this woman was involved with King Solomon do you?" I ask.

"Well... it's not that hard to fathom," the Professor says, leaning back in his chair. "The man had seven hundred wives."

"And half that in concubines," Dr Cooke adds.

"I'm not sure he would've had much time to be at the mines with all those women," the Professor looks at Dr Cooke in wonder. "I'm surprised he was ever able to leave the bed chamber."

"As intriguing as it is, there are no markings I can see on the grave site," I say, pulling the paper so close to my nose it is nearly touching.

"And there are no annotations of markings," Dr Cooke says, reading the paper of the findings. "They were very thorough and don't have a clue who she was either."

I study the photograph of the crude grave for another minute before putting it down.

"While interesting, I don't think it's the answer we are looking for," I say, picking up another paper and reading.

The shadows in the room get darker as night falls, and I

push my glasses up to rub my tired eyes.

"We've been at it for hours, June," the Professor says, his eyes half closed with fatigue. "We've been through everything twice. There's no marking here."

I sigh, looking at the jumble of paperwork strewn across the table.

"You're right," I sigh, and then suddenly slam my first to the table. "I could have sworn I was right. I would have staked my *life* that sign meant something. But it's all codswallop. The boat was probably just travelling upstream, that's why the marking was on the stone."

Griffin's head pokes out of the bedroom door, his hair sticking up at the back where it must have been resting on the headboard while he wrote.

"Everything alright?" he asks.

No, I want to scream, *nothing is alright!* I am stuck in a country with a dangerous mob after me because I'm meant to know the location to a priceless artefact that I've somehow convinced myself exists with only the flimsiest information. What was I possibly thinking? I look down again at the piece of paper that we bought off Quinn. It probably means nothing. I've become obsessed with something because a seedy, desperate man convinced me it was something so I would give him money to pay off his gambling debt. How could I have been so stupid? How could I have been so illogical?

I laugh and shake my head.

"Why did I get so caught up on a word written on a piece of paper that I bought from some *charlatan*," I ask, throwing my arms up in the air.

Clint comes out of his own bedroom, rubbing the side of his face, still half asleep.

"What's going on? What was the noise?" he asks.

"It was reality coming crashing down on me," I say, shaking my head. "A heavy dose that this was all just a bloody waste of time."

"Didn't find anything?" Griffin asks, and his look of sympathy gets me on my feet.

I start roughly collecting the papers, not bothering to do a neat job of it.

"There's nothing to find," I say, gathering all the papers into my arms and bringing them to my chest. "Honestly, a magical ring…"

I walk over to the bin and unceremoniously jam all of the paperwork into it.

"Complete waste of time," I breathe.

Chapter Twelve

"You have everything?" Griffin asks me, flashing me a kind smile.

I return it before nodding.

"I'll be pleased to see the back of this place," Dr Cooke says, jamming his hat on his head.

The woman behind the reception desk tightens her mouth, clearly offended, but says nothing.

"Has Calvin taken my humidifier to the car?" the Professor asks, scanning the floor by our feet.

"Clint just took the last suitcase to the car. Omar's waiting outside to take us to the airport," I explain.

"Right, well, I'll just go and check he hasn't put it at the bottom. I don't want it to get squished," the Professor says.

"I better go and make sure he doesn't wander off," Dr Cooke says before turning and following the Professor out of the hotel.

"Here is your paperwork," the receptionist says, handing Griffin his receipt. "We hope to see you again soon."

I pick up my bag and take Griffin's outstretched hand.

"Not bloody likely," he mutters, and squeezes my hand as we walk across the lobby.

"You alright?" he asks me, and I look up into his concerned face.

"Fine," I say, shrugging. "I'm just sorry I dragged us all here for nothing."

"It wasn't nothing," Griffin says. "You've given Simon his little exposé, so you're off the hook."

I smile noncommittally as Griffin opens the hotel door.

I know Simon is not going to be pleased with what we've got, because we don't have anything. We have a nice little tour of a museum anyone could look up online and some footage of the bank of the Nile River in the dark. I'm not sure we will be making the six o'clock news with that.

I go through the door Griffin hold open and blink once, trying to adjust my eyes to bright sun.

I can't see the van out front anywhere so I turn around to look at Griffin.

"Did you say—"

A hand covers my mouth. My eyes widen and look to Griffin who wears the same surprised look on his face.

Griffin yells my name, trying to reach out for me, but a man grabs his arms from behind his back.

The man is wearing all black and is much larger than Griffin, but it doesn't stop Griffin from struggling against his hold.

The man who is covering my mouth has me in a vice lock grip, holding my middle so tightly I can barely breathe.

Another man wearing all black approaches Griffin and lands a hard blow against his jaw. Griffin's head lolls to the side in a state of unconsciousness.

"Griffin!" I scream through the hand over my mouth, but barely make a sound.

I'm pulled backwards, my feet dragging on the ground as I try desperately to break free.

I hear the sound of a car door open and I'm shoved in sideways, my balance causing me to fall onto the back seat.

"What the hell do you think—" I scream the moment my mouth is free, but I'm cut off by the slamming of the car's door. My legs push up to my stomach from the force.

A man stares at me, sitting on a bench style seat across from me, his back facing the driver.

"Go," he says calmly and I feel the car pull away.

I sit up quickly, pressing my back to the cold leather seat. We are in some sort of large SUV. The man across from me has his legs crossed, his hands clasped together on his knee. He studies me with an eerie sense of calm, and I find his attitude chilling.

"Who are you? What the hell is going on?" I say, trying to keep my voice steady.

I look at the door handle, but the car is moving at an incredible speed considering we are in the city. Even if I was able to open the door without this man stopping me,

I'm not sure I would survive the fall.

"There is no point in trying to escape," the man says, his voice so smooth it is almost cathartic.

"Who are you?" I repeat my earlier question. "And what do you want?"

"My name is Ahmed Gamal," he says, tilting his head to the side. "And I want a moment of your time."

So this is Ahmed Gamal. He looks younger than I thought he would be, but as I study his face I can see the tautness of his skin, and realise he must have had some work done. Though he hasn't bothered to cover the grey in his black hair. His light grey suit and buttoned down white shirt project an air of ease, but I can tell by his unnervingly calm attitude it is all a façade.

"My time?" I ask, confused. "My time for what?"

"For your... expertise," he says, playing with his word choice.

"I—I don't see how I can be of any help to you," I say.

He raises an eyebrow.

"Don't you?" he asks.

We study each other for a moment and I refuse to flinch.

If I'm going to die at the hands of the Egyptian mob, by God I'm going to go down with my dignity.

Or at least my own deluded sense of dignity.

"You have been looking for something that greatly interests me," Ahmed says, uncrossing his legs and leaning forward.

"I… I don't know what you are talking about," I lift my chin defiantly.

"Come, let's not play games," Ahmed says, smiling. "There's no need to make this… unpleasant."

"Unpleasant?" I let out a short laugh. "I suppose you kidnapping me and assaulting my boyfriend was supposed to come across as friendly was it?"

Ahmed nods once, still smiling.

"I apologise. My men, they can be a bit… shall we say, tactless?"

The lack of even a morsel of regret in his voice sets my teeth on edge.

"What makes you think, even if I *could*, I would be willing to help you?" I say, the disgust evident in my voice.

"When I want something, I find I can be… persuasive," Ahmed says.

"Well, I'm not easily persuaded," I say, folding my trembling arms over my chest.

Ahmed studies me for a moment, and for a split second I see something that almost looks like respect on his face.

"Your spirit is admirable," Ahmed nods. "Foolish, but admirable."

"What do you want?" I ask.

His smile slips for a moment and I can tell he is not used to being spoken to this way.

Quite frankly, I'm not sure where this bravado is

coming from as I'm not sure I'd even be able to stand on my shaky legs right now.

"The ring of Solomon," he says, his eyes unblinking. "Where is it?"

I pause for a moment, wondering how best to handle this. My heart pounds in my chest. I could play coy, but then he might think I know something that I don't.

"I don't know where it is," I say emphatically. "From what I've seen I'm not sure it even exists."

"Oh, it exists," Ahmed says, leaning back in his seat.

"And how do you know that for certain?" I ask sceptically.

"Because history tells us it does," he answers.

I snort in derision again.

"No, it doesn't. It speculates of it, at best," I say, shaking my head.

"You don't believe the stories? I'm surprised," he says.

"There are stories about Leprechauns at the end of a rainbow," I say, my mouth twisting. "I certainly don't expect to find a pot of gold when it rains."

"Yes, but when the stories have tangible evidence, you put stock in them, no?" Ahmed says.

"And what tangible evidence do you have that such a ring exists—or ever existed?" I ask.

Ahmed brushes his finger across his lips, and waits.

I can tell he is debating what to tell me, and the fact that he does know *something* makes me lean forward.

I'm always curious. Even in the most terrifying scenario.

What does he know?

"I have spent my life in the pursuit of learning all that I can about my homeland," Ahmed says, holding his hands out wide. "Egypt is a country with deep and fascinating roots. As I accumulated wealth, I also accumulated power. And with that power, I find I want to learn more about those who also had power and ruled over this beautiful land. I feel a certain… *kinship* to them."

I say nothing but continue to stare.

"King Solomon was one of the wealthiest men that ever lived. He had the power of wealth, the favour of God, and the respect of his people," he continues. "I have spent the better part of two decades learning about his life."

"It's a shame in all of that study you were only able to emulate the wealth," I say coolly.

A flash of anger crosses his face, and he reaches in his pocket for his phone.

"I take it you are attached to your boyfriend, Ms Jenson? You came here with your grandfather as well, no?"

My face pales.

"Don't test my patience. You won't like the results," he says, tapping a finger to the top on his phone.

"If you lay one single finger on them—" I threaten.

"You will do nothing, because you *can't* do anything to me," he says, smirking. "Now, back to the ring."

"I don't know where the bloody ring is," I say, throwing my arms in the air. "I know just as much about that god-forsaken thing as you do."

"Oh, I doubt that," Ahmed says, nonplussed with my outburst. "As I said, I have spent the better part of twenty years acquiring lost artefacts of King Solomon. I feel I know a great deal more than you do about it."

"What are you talking about?" I ask, frowning.

"I know you have the paper which was taken from me," he says, studying my reaction.

"You can have it," I say, shaking my head. "It won't do you any good, though. It means nothing."

"I doubt that," he says.

"You have a map to the ring, do you? And that's just the last missing piece?" I ask.

"It might be," he says, pursing his lips. "Like I said, I have many artefacts from King Solomon which are not known to the Egyptian museum. I am confident that they will lead me in the direction I need to go."

I narrow my eyes momentarily at his choice of words. Does he really have what is needed to follow the clues to get the lost ring? Does he know the clue I have is a direction?

But he donated the granite rock. Surely if he knew it had a clue on it he never would have risked its discovery in the public eye.

"You have the clue on you?" he asks.

My hand instinctively moves to my bag where the clue is tucked away and I groan at my mistake.

"I didn't mean that to be a question," he says, the side of his mouth lifting in a smirk. "I knew you wouldn't leave it to someone else, whether you put stock in it or not."

"What are you going to do with the ring, if you find it?" I ask, my hand still on my knapsack.

My question gives him pause for a moment, before he shrugs.

"Possess it," he says calmly.

I frown at his words.

"We are not dissimilar, you and I," he says. "We both have a profound love for history."

I study him for a moment, my hand still on my bag.

"I want the clue now," he says, picking up his phone and running his thumb across the screen. "Don't make me ask again."

I look at the phone, my nose flaring, then I open my bag. I take out the small piece of paper and hand it to him.

He looks at it for a brief moment before slipping it into the inside his jacket pocket.

"Now what?" I ask.

"Now, you go home," Ahmed says, and knocks once on the glass separating us from the driver.

"Home?" I ask, raising my eyebrows.

"I don't need you," he says, shaking his head.

"But—you're just going to let me go?" I ask

incredulously.

"A dead Englishwoman is not going to help me find the ring, and I expect the people who sent you here would notice if you went missing. That is not the sort of international attention I want to surround myself or the search for the ring with," he says.

"But, how do you know I won't get out of this car and tell the government what you are after?" I ask him.

"Because they won't believe you," he says.

"Oh no?" I ask. "And why's that?"

Honestly, I don't know why I am even asking this. He's letting me go, and my brain is screaming at my mouth to shut up! But there is something about his arrogance that goes against my better judgment.

"Because I am Ahmed Gamal," he simply states.

I feel the car lurch to a stop and look outside the window to see we are back out front of the shabby hotel.

I reach for the handle, and when no one stops me I push the door open.

"I meant what I said, Ms Jenson," Ahmed says and I pause from climbing out to look back at him. "We are not unalike, you and I."

"We are nothing alike," I spit out, shaking my head. "I want to understand history, and you want to possess something that will never truly belong to you."

"We shall see."

And then he is gone.

Chapter Thirteen

"Oh, God! Are you alright?" I ask, grasping Griffin's swollen face between my hands.

"I'm fine," Griffin mumbles through a fat lip, and pulls me into his arms. "Are *you* alright?"

"What did they do to you? Where did they take you?" Dr Cooke asks, trying to get a good look at me.

"We just went for a drive," I say, shaking my head. "It was Ahmed Gamal. He just wanted the clue. He made me give it to him."

"You did the right thing, June Bug" the Professor says, his face drained of colour. "We're archaeologists, not bloody James Bond."

"Christ, when they took you," Griffin says, and I can feel his arms shaking. "I woke up to the Professor shaking me. They left me in the alley behind the hotel."

"It looks like you had a rougher time than I did," I put my fingertips to Griffin's split lip and he winces.

"Looks worse then it is, I'm sure," Griffin says, putting his hand to his ribs.

We stand quietly for a moment, gathering ourselves.

"Oh, June, you're back," Clint says, offering me a smile

as he comes around the corner of the building, tucking his phone into his pant's pocket.

"She's *back?*" Griffin says in outrage. "She was bloody abducted, you twat!"

The smile falls off Clint's face.

"Alright, no need to have a go at me!" he says.

"I'll have more than a bloody go in a minute," Griffin says, releasing me and taking a step closer to Clint. "You and that bloody boss of yours—Sending us to a bloody war torn country for some stupid piece of paper that means absolutely nothing. Then his so called contact sends the bloody Egyptian mob after us—"

"You know, I didn't sign up for this either," Clint says, throwing his arms in the air. "I wanted to be a *director* for Christ's sake. Then I get assigned to this as a 'temporary assignment' which *never* ends, and quite frankly it's not all that it's cracked up to be."

"I—you—*what?*" Griffin yells.

"Yeah, that's right. I've got two blokes who think I'm at their bloody beck and call all day long—one of whom can't even remember my bleedin' name!" Clint yells, pointing to the Professor who looks around to see if there is someone behind him. "Following you lot around, risking my neck every five minutes…"

"Risking your—" Griffin sputters, turning to me. "I'll kill him. I'm going to *bloody kill him!*"

"Before you kill anyone, can we please go home?" I ask

him, feeling beyond tired.

"Er—there might be a slight problem with that…" Clint hedges.

"What now?" Dr Cooke asks warily. "Don't tell me the airport is closed again."

"No, it's open," Clint says. "We just can't go there yet."

"Why not?" I ask.

"That was Simon on the phone," Clint says, pointing to the phone in his pocket. "We need to go back to the museum and film the conclusion before we can go home."

"Absolutely not," Griffin says, taking my hand. "We are leaving. Simon can take a long walk."

"How can he expect us to film anything after what just happened?" I ask.

"He can't, it's preposterous," Dr Cooke says, nervously turning his hat in his hands. "Can we please just get in the car so Omar can take us to the airport?"

"Oh, yes, our heroic armed guard," Griffin snorts, and then winces from the pain in causes. "Where was he when June was being abducted and I was beaten to a pulp."

"Er—yes, well, that might have been *slightly* my fault," the Professor says, scratching the side of his head. "I was just having him install the humidifier in the van when it all went down, I'm afraid."

We all stare at the Professor and he at least has the decency to look embarrassed.

"Let's just forget it and go home," I suggest.

"June, I really don't think that's something you want to do," Clint hedges.

I raise my eyebrows.

"You see, I mentioned to Simon that once you had returned—"

"Returned from being abducted?" Griffin interrupts.

"Yes," Clint nods. "Well, I told Simon you all might not be feeling up to filming anything else."

"And?" I ask.

"And he mentioned something about your contract. Something about suing for breach. And he also mentioned that your deal would be off," Clint says, counting the points on his fingers.

"He can't sue us for breach! No one would agree for us to put our lives in danger," I argue.

"Well, Simon says that we have footage of you already in the museum, which was your consent that it was a safe place to film," Clint says, shrugging.

"What deal have you made with Simon?" Griffin frowns at me.

"He must be referring to the renegotiations," I mutter, trying to wrap my head around all of this.

I know exactly what Simon will do if we return without the footage he wants. He wouldn't think twice about trying to sue us. I don't think he would win, but it would definitely drag us all through the mud. Innocent or not, we would be at the centre of a scandal again. I spent the better part of my life living under that cloud. Do I really want that? Do I want to put the Professor through that again—all the media attention and reporters trying to get our side of the story?

And what about the life I have negotiated for us all after this is done? We have all worked so hard. How can I let us walk away with nothing? The Professor and Dr Cooke, they deserve a lovely retirement where they can make jam all day and get on each other's nerves. Griffin has worked hard for his playwright success, what would a lawsuit do to his career? Maybe people would avoid working with him, not wanting the association. I know all too well how that feels.

"Would it be so bad if we just stopped at the museum to film the conclusion?" I ask, turning to the others.

"You can't be serious?" Griffin shakes his head.

"Griffin, I know Simon. He will do exactly what Clint has just said. He doesn't care about us, he cares about the story," I argue.

"Let him sue us!" Griffin yells. "Let's see what the British public make of him forcing us into unsafe work environments."

"And they will probably side with us," I agree. "But some will call us weak. Some will praise us. Some will volunteer to take our place. We will receive every possible reaction, and be on the front of every tabloid by the week end. I don't want to do that all over again. Do you?"

I turn to look at Dr Cooke and the Professor, who both look wary at the prospect of the media attention.

"It will take an hour, tops," I assure Griffin.

"And if Ahmed Gamal finds out you haven't left Egypt?" Dr Cooke asks.

"He won't," I say. "And anyways, he has the clue, he doesn't need anything from me anymore."

"That's the spirit," Clint smiles, but it falters at our disgusted looks at him.

"Er—I'll just wait in the car with Omar, I think," he says, and scrambles off down the alleyway to the front of the hotel.

"You know, I'm starting to dislike Craig," the Professor says, following after Clint.

Chapter Fourteen

"I know I sound like a broken record…" Griffin says, climbing the sleek marbled stairs of the Cairo museum.

"I know. You don't like this." I squeeze his hand. "We go straight to the airport after this. It will be over in no time."

"Unless some nutter sets off another bomb," the Professor says, and his voice echoes around the large atrium.

"Can you please not say the word *bomb* in the museum?" Dr Cooke hisses, his eyes darting over the banister rail to below. "I don't particularly want to get arrested and have a cavity search."

"Soon we will be back home, back to our normal lives," I say, offering Griffin a smile.

He smiles, but it quickly falters as he brings his hand to his face, grimacing from his now red and swollen lip.

"Since when has our life ever been normal?" he asks.

"Good point," I concede.

Once at the top of the staircase we turn left and re-enter the Tutankhamun exhibit.

"Wasn't this on display at the Ashmolean when we

met?" Griffin asks, pointing to the tomb of King Tut, the golden perfection shining brightly under the spotlight.

"Yes, it was on loan," I nod.

"It was meant to go to America next I believe," Dr Cooke says, studying the tomb. "But after the recent discoveries the Egyptians wanted him returned."

"Well, can you blame them?" the Professor asks, peering through the glass at the golden chariot fabric displayed in the cases. "If we've learned anything while being here it is that the Americans cannot be trusted with… well, anything."

"Why did it need to be returned here?" Griffin asks.

"They performed further scans on King Tut's resting place and have discovered hidden chambers through the thermal scans," I say, joining the Professor at the large circular display.

"Hidden chambers?" Griffin says, his eyebrows raised. "Why aren't we on that assignment?"

"My lad, it is one of the most coveted archaeological sites of our time," Dr Cooke says, snorting. "You'd have to be the bloody Sean Connery of archaeology to get on that site."

"And we are, what, exactly?" Griffin asks.

"Rowan Atkinson" the Professor says.

"You know, what we do matters just as much as those on the ground, tools in hand," I say, shaking my head.

"Really?" Dr Cooke says. "I thought we were more of

the Cilla Black variety."

"We bring history to people in a relatable way," I say, trying to convince them. "We encourage people watching to find a love and passion for things of the past. History is one of the dying arts. Who knows how many we have inspired to study history for themselves?"

"You think we inspire people?" Griffin asks.

"Yes, and then they will get to go and be the next Sean Connery of archaeology," I say, smiling at the Professor.

"What do they think are in the hidden chambers of his tomb?" Griffin asks.

"Well they never found the sarcophagus. Or Nefertiti, his stepmother, the infamous Queen of Egypt," I explain. "I think the hopes are that she could be buried in one of the hidden chambers."

"Why would his stepmother be buried with him?" Griffin asks.

"His whole family—his grandparents, parents, wife, their two children—they were all buried in his tomb. Nefertiti was the prestigious second wife to King Tut's father, and together they ruled Egypt. It is even thought that she ruled by herself for a time, right after Tut's father died, before Tutankhamun became Pharaoh. King Tut was married to their child—essentially his half sister."

"Ugh," Clint exclaims, the first reminder he is even in the room since we arrived. He leans against the wall with his arms crossed. "That's disgusting."

"Not unheard of for most of history," Dr Cooke says. "Family trees were very small and tightly woven."

"Yes, fascinating," Clint says, his head leaning against a display case. "Can we please just film this stupid conclusion and get the hell out of here?"

I'm not sure he's taken kindly to the silent treatment he's received from the group since the car ride over.

I study Clint's petulant expression and have to bite my tongue. I know he isn't the entire reason for us having to do this, but in this case I am more than happy to shoot the messenger.

"Why don't you do something useful and get the camera rolling?" I ask, walking past the display cases towards the Tanis exhibit. "Come on, let's get this over with."

I walk to the doorway and stop as a bright light blinds my vision.

Chapter Fifteen

"So sorry about that," Thomas says, walking over to me, smiling. "We've been taking some pictures for the article, and were just capturing this remarkable granite piece."

I look to my direct right and see the petroglyph with the hieroglyphic etched on the boat.

"So you *are* here for a story," I say, turning my gaze back to him.

His wife Carolyn lowers her long lens camera and smiles at me in sincere apology.

She just seems so... nice. What in the world is she doing with Thomas?

"Tom here is writing a series of articles about our honeymoon travels for the BBC," she says, the pride evident in her voice.

"Is he now?" I raise my eyebrows. "You think he would be too busy *enjoying* his honeymoon to spend it working."

"Multitasking is my middle name," Tom laughs and his wife joins in.

"And what sort of article are you writing about the

Tanis Pharaohs?" I ask, causally making my way closer, the others following behind me.

"Oh, June, a journalist never gives away his story," Thomas says, tapping the side of his nose with his finger.

I look at Carolyn, who smiles at Thomas, but I see for just a split second that her smile falters.

Either she doesn't agree with what Thomas is doing, or he's lying.

The odds are pretty fair either way, considering the person he is.

"So you are taking pictures in here, then?" I ask his wife. "That's a lovely camera. Are you a photographer?"

"Yes, actually," she says. "I used to do weddings, but since Tom and I have been together I've switched to photojournalism."

"Right." I look around the room. "I saw you were taking a picture of that petroglyph before."

"Oh yes, the lighting in here picks up the engravings beautifully," she says. "Would you like to see?"

"Oh, I'm sure June doesn't want to—" Thomas starts.

I put my hand behind my back and hook my index finger, hoping Griffin gets the hint.

"Did you say you came from Thailand?" Griffin asks, stepping past me to stand by Thomas. "Did you ride on the elephants there?"

"Er—no. What happened to your face?" Thomas asks, trying to look past Griffin as I walk over to Carolyn.

"Walked into a pole. We had a go trying to ride the elephants in Thailand, but Dr Cooke couldn't get on, and then the Professor wandered off..."

"That's a shame," Thomas says, still trying to look past Griffin and failing.

"They were bloody massive, weren't they, Albert?" Dr Cooke asks, shaking his head. "Though we got to bathe them in the mud, didn't we?"

Griffin says something else, but I don't listen now that I have Carolyn on my own.

"June, I do want to apologise for Tom's behaviour to you and your family in the past," Carolyn says, placing her hand on my arm in a friendly manner. "I know it is hard to believe, but he really has changed. He is kind and wonderful, and I know he feels terribly embarrassed about his past transgressions."

"Does he?" I ask.

"He would tell you so himself," she nods.

"Is that a Nikon?" I ask, hoping to change the subject. I point to her camera, even though it has Nikon written across the front of the lens.

"Yes! Tom got it for me for our wedding," she beams. "Do you have one?"

"Er—nothing that fancy I'm afraid," I say. "It's more of a hobby for me. But I have been thinking of investing in a really good one to take with me to excavation sites."

"You'll want to take some classes too; lighting can be

tricky," she says and I thank my stars for the opening.

"Does this one take nice pictures of artefacts then?" I ask, trying to sound nonchalant.

I can hear Dr Cooke and Griffin still talking animatedly, effectively keeping Thomas away.

"Oh, beautiful ones. Would you like to see?" she asks.

I nod my head and peer over her shoulder.

"See how it picks up the deep lines in the engravings?" she says in excitement. "It's amazing to think of how they did such beautiful work with simple hand tools."

"You sound like me," I say, jokingly. But then I frown slightly. She actually does sound like me.

"Oh, let me show you a picture I took in Jerusalem yesterday—the lighting was just amazing. I got the buried wall *right* at sunset," she flips through the pictures and then turns the camera for me to see.

"You went to Jerusalem yesterday?" I ask, keeping my voice light. "You really are getting around on this honeymoon."

"Work seems to make Tom happy," she says, and looks over my shoulder in Thomas' direction.

God, she is just smitten. Here she is, on her honeymoon, and he has her traipsing all over Egypt and beyond for a story.

Oh God, I think I actually feel sorry for this woman.

I study the picture on the camera. It's a shot of the wall they uncovered where King Solomon built his temple.

She is a very talented photographer, I have to give her that. She's captured the wall with the orange sun setting in the background, turning the desert sand into a sparkling pool of reflection.

She is taking pictures of things linked to King Solomon.

And now he has her taking picture in the Tanis exhibit.

He must know the rumoured connection between the two, which means he is doing a story on King Solomon. But what story?

"Oh, there's an amazing one with Tom on a camel," she says, and starts flipping through the camera.

There are more close-ups of the rock wall outside of Jerusalem, the Nile River, and a round rock burial ground.

"That rock formation," I say, pointing to the camera and she stops scrolling. "Where did you see that?"

"Timna, I believe," she says, studying the photo. "I got some really amazing shots of the mines."

She slides to the next picture and my heart stops.

"It's amazing how people without any sort of machinery could build and work these mines. We did a tour of the pyramids, and it was a sight to behold. You should really go and take a tour while you are still here," she smiles.

I can barely move, and I force myself to look up at her words.

"Er—yes, absolutely," I nod.

"Darling, you haven't been giving the plot away, I hope," Thomas says, coming to stand beside Carolyn and wrapping his arm around her shoulders.

"Not at all, just showing June this amazing camera you bought me," she says beaming at him.

My heart is beating fast in my chest. I want to leave, I want to be alone to think about the millions of things that are racing through my head right now. I can't let Thomas know I have figured it out. That I have seen it.

How much does he know?

"When are you leaving Egypt?" I ask, looking between them. I want to sound casual but I know my question came out fast and rude.

Griffin stands beside me, putting his hand on the small of my back.

"We haven't quite wrapped things up here," Thomas says, smiling at me. "Playing it by ear, I guess you'd say."

"Hopefully not too long," Carolyn says, smiling in exasperation. "We need to get back to the *relaxing* aspect of our honeymoon."

God, she is so nice. I look at Thomas' smug face and my mind quickly tries to justify letting him get his comeuppance. But then I look at the sweet face of his wife, his poor unsuspecting wife, with her massive diamond ring and naive outlook on life, and I just can't do it to her.

"Thomas, you're not working with Ahmed Gamal, are you?" I ask, and watch as his eyes widen slightly in confirmation as the last puzzle piece falls into place in my mind.

"Who?" he hedges, but I see through the lie immediately.

"Thomas, you have to listen to me. He is not a man you want to align yourself with. He's dangerous, and ruthless—"

"Honestly June, I don't know who you are talking about," he laughs.

"For Christ's sake, listen to me," I implore. "Whatever it is he wants from you, whatever you've promised him for your next big story—he's just using you."

"June," his smile falters. "With all due respect, you don't know what you're talking about."

"Do you honestly think once he has the artefact he is going to let you live to tell the story? The Egyptian government would *never* allow him to keep such a piece—the law here is that lost treasures belong to the country. He wouldn't find it just to give it up," I exclaim, imploring him to see reason.

"June, you have never understood the importance of the story," he shakes his head. "What it takes to survive in this industry. Sometimes you have to do things that are... regrettable."

"We aren't talking about you betraying someone for a good scoop here," I say, shaking my head. "That just makes you an asshole. But aligning yourself with a murderer who will stop at nothing to get what he wants? That makes you suicidal."

"Tom?" Carolyn looks at him with worry etched across her face.

"It will be fine," he smiles at her.

"No it won't, I promise you," I say, turning my gaze to Carolyn. "If Thomas won't listen to reason, I hope you will. What you are doing is both stupid and dangerous. No story is worth losing your life over."

"Would you please stop scaring my wife!" Thomas snaps, raising his voice. "You have no clue what you are talking about!"

"Yes, I do!" I argue. "Look at Griffin's face, Thomas. You think he walked into a pole? Ahmed Gamal's men beat him up and abducted me because I had a piece of paper he wanted."

"Tom, I think you should listen to her," Carolyn says, taking a step back.

"That's enough!" Tom says, taking his wife's hand. "We are leaving."

"Finally, you are talking sense," I say.

"We are leaving the museum, not Egypt," Tom says, narrowing his eyes. "I know what you're doing, June. Thought you would finally pay me back after all these years, did you?"

"What?" I frown.

"You know as well as I do, that this is the story of a

lifetime—for both of us. Now I extended the olive branch and asked you to work on it with me but you refused. Don't try and scare me off because you regret that I have an advantage over you," he says.

"An advantage?" I say, shaking my head. "Haven't you been listening? Ahmed Gamal is not an advantage—he's a death sentence."

"Tom, I want to go home!" Carolyn whimpers, trying to tug her hand free.

"Would you stop! Can't you see what she is doing?" Thomas asks, shaking his head. "We are so close, and you want to quit now?"

"Not if it means risking our lives," she says to him, the tears welling in her eyes.

Tom studies her for a moment.

"I'm disappointed. I thought you were made of tougher stuff then this, Carolyn," he says.

She cries out before wrenching her hand free and walks out of the exhibit without another word.

"Thomas, it's not worth your life. Your future," I say, shaking my head.

"I won't stop chasing the story, June. It's not who I am. And I didn't think it was who you are, either." He turns on his heel, and storms after his wife.

Chapter Sixteen

"Let's get out of here," Griffin says, grabbing my hand. "If Simon doesn't like what we've got he knows what he can do."

"We can't go," I say, shaking my head.

"What? Why?" Griffin asks.

"Because I've found the next clue," I reveal.

"What? Where?" Dr Cooke says, looking around the exhibit.

"Not here, it's in Timna," I explain. "It was on Carolyn's camera."

"What was?" Dr Cooke asks.

"Beside where the bones of that woman were found. Remember, you showed me the picture?" I ask to the Professor.

"But there were no markings on the site," Dr Cooke argues.

"It wasn't on the grave, that's why I didn't see it. About twenty feet from the grave was the marking for the mine. The sign the Egyptians engraved at the opening was etched with the word *down*. When you look at the grave and then the sign—the way it lines up looks just like a tombstone!" I feel an eerie chill run up my spine.

"Oh June," Griffin says, running his hand through his hair. "What makes you think that's the next clue? It's just some bloody sign!"

"It isn't," I argue.

"How do you know? There has to be the 'down' hieroglyphic carved in different places all over Egypt," he argues.

"Because that woman was linked to King Solomon," I explain. "She was found at his mine—but she should never have been there."

"It's a coincidence," Griffin argues.

"No, it's not. And Ahmed Gamal knows it too," I say. "That's why he sent Thomas there."

"All the more reason to get out of here!" Griffin yells. "Let him have the bloody ring, or whatever it is that clue leads to. It's not worth it."

"I can't," I say, shaking my head. "I can't let a man like that have it."

"Well, I can!" Clint says, shoving his camera into his bag. "I didn't sign up for this shit—I certainly am not willing to die for it. I'll make up some bloody conclusion and film it myself!"

"Clarence, you're not leaving, are you?" the Professor says, taking out his journal from his coat pocket. "Only, I had a few errands I needed doing."

"Do them yourself!" Clint yells, lifting his bag further

up his shoulder. "You know, I don't even think I *like* history."

He turns and storms out of the exhibit.

"June," Dr Cooke carefully interjects. "There are people all over the world that possess black market artefacts. You cannot possibly hope to rescue them all."

"Probably not," I agree. "But I can rescue this one. I can make this right."

Griffin sighs.

"Why do you think you have to *fix* everything? Solve the world's problems?" Griffin yells in exasperation. "You just got through telling Thomas to go home and forget it, but you want to stay? You think you owe something, but you don't!"

"I do! I do owe something—to all of you," I say, throwing my arms up in the air. "Because it is all of my fault."

"What are you talking about?" Griffin asks.

"Why we have to do this—why we even have to be here. It's all my fault, don't you see?" I ask, looking from Griffin to the Professor. "If I hadn't introduced Thomas into our lives, he never would have been able to sell the Professor's story. He would have been able to retire in peace. And you Dr Cooke—well, we never would have lost those years."

"June, my dear—" Dr Cooke starts.

"And if I hadn't dragged you all to Colorado and

pretended I was commissioned for that dig, I would still have my position at the University and we wouldn't have to do this bloody television program," I say.

The Professor watches me carefully.

"Griffin, you could be writing your plays," I say turning back to him. "The Professor and Dr Cooke could be retired and making jam right now."

I stare at the ground.

"Well, that's a lot to take in," Dr Cooke says, wiping his brow with his handkerchief.

"You've really fallen down the rabbit hole this time, haven't you, June Bug?" the Professor asks, taking a seat on a bench along the far wall.

"I just want to fix it," I implore them to understand.

"And how do you suppose you are going to do that?" the Professor asks.

"Simon says if I can just give him a solid theory, he'll make sure you all have everything you need. He's not going to want a theory of something that's already been found, legally or not, when we weren't the ones to find it." I explain.

"But, we already do," Griffin says, frowning at me.

"We already do, what?" I ask.

"We already have everything we need. We don't need Simon for that," he says.

"What?" I ask again. "What are you talking about? You want to write—"

"Of course I want to write," Griffin says. "I also want to go to China and not fall down a man hole. I'd like to go to Scotland and not be pushed in the lake to test whether the Loch Ness Monster exists."

He looks to Dr Cooke and the Professor who are both sitting on the bench, chuckling.

"But, that's not life, is it?" Griffin asks me.

"But it could be," I argue, taking a step towards him. "If I just do this one last thing—"

"It won't ever be," Griffin says, taking my hand. "Because that's not *real*, June. Life isn't neat and orderly and perfect. Life is this. Me and you and the Professor and Dr Cooke. It's adventure and mayhem and messy and wonderful. It will never go the way you plan it, and I think if it does… well… that would actually be a pretty *boring* life, wouldn't it?"

"But, before, in England. You said you wanted to write," I argue.

"I want to do a lot of things, and I will, one day," Griffin says. "But most importantly, I want do them with you, which will be a little hard if we're all dead."

"June, you didn't make Thomas go to those newspapers, just like you didn't make me stop defending my friend when he needed me the most," Dr Cooke says, putting his hand on the Professor's knee and offering him a smile. "You give yourself too much responsibility by taking on the actions of others, when they are no one's but their own."

"And you and I never would have met if you hadn't joined that fake Alliance," Griffin says.

"Oh good Lord, I forgot about the Alliance!" the Professor laughs.

Dr Cooke joins him, wiping tears from his own eyes.

I can't help the smile that tugs at my cheeks. That was one of my more stupid moments in life.

"And we wouldn't have been able to right a terrible injustice to a fine historian," Dr Cooke says, looking to the Professor.

"And we wouldn't have found the lost treasure of Butch Cassidy," Griffin says, squeezing my hand.

"And we never would have met Clarence," the Professor says.

"Clint," Dr Cooke, Griffin, and I correct him in unison.

"The point is," the Professor says, standing up and walking towards me. "Never be sorry for the things you did in life, June. Save all the regret for the things you never even considered doing."

I reach my hand out to touch his arm, and lean forward to place a kiss on his cheek.

"I'm so proud that you're my grandfather," I whisper in his ear before drawing back.

"Who wouldn't be?" he winks.

"Well, now that we have that sorted, what are we going to do?" Dr Cooke asks, standing and joining the group in the centre of the room. "The airport is open. We could be on the next plane out of here."

"Thomas is going to lead Ahmed Gamal right to that ring," I say. "He has all the information, it's only a matter of time before they piece it together."

"If you want to go after the ring, I'll follow you," Griffin says, reaching for my hand. "But if we're going into the Lion's Den I want to make sure it's because you want to, not because you have some deluded notion that you *have* to."

"I vote we go and find it," the Professor says, readjusting his hat. "I'm not letting that tosser, Thomas, get another leg up on me."

"If we find it before Thomas does though, I think Gamal will kill him," I say, biting my bottom lip.

"June, whether he finds the ring or not is inconsequential. He's a dead man, anyways," the Professor says.

"What do you think?" I ask, turning to Griffin.

He studies me for a moment before nodding.

"Who knows, I might find another black eye to complete the set," he says, pointing up to his swollen face.

"We're all in," Dr Cooke says, coming to stand beside the Professor. "We're all certifiably *insane*, but we're in."

I scan their faces.

"Thank you," I say.

"So where are we off to?" Griffin says.

"If we think the grave site is where the next clue is, we need to go to Timna," the Professor says, bringing out his journal.

"Do you think that is where Thomas is heading?" Griffin asks me.

"Assuming he doesn't back off," I nod.

"I don't know about you, but the wife is the one I find unnerving," Dr Cooke mock shudders. "No one is *that* pleasant."

"And did you hear how she pronounced Jerusalem?" Griffin snorts and then winces at the pain in his face. "Who does she think she is, the bloody Queen of Sheba?"

I begin to laugh, but the smile fades from my face.

"What?" Griffin asks, looking concerned. "What is it?"

I turn to look at him, a look of amazement on my face.

"Griffin," I say, momentarily stunned. "You're *brilliant.*"

.

Chapter Seventeen

In a hotel room across from the museum the four of us pore over the paperwork spread out on the floor in front of the television.

"I still don't know how we are going to find a little ring by sitting here and staring at pictures," Griffin sighs, shaking his head.

"Because we are missing something," I explain, my eyes not leaving the photographs. "I know we are! I just can't *see* it."

Griffin picks up the photograph of the gravesite in Timna where the lower half of the woman and her unborn child was found.

"So, you think this woman is…" Griffin starts.

"The Queen of Sheba," I nod.

"June, dear, I know I sound like a broken record, but that's a bit of a stretch," Dr Cooke says.

"But it isn't, not if you think about everything we know about the bones," I argue. "A woman—even if she was one of the King's wives or concubines, would not have been at that mine. The only people that would've been there were the mine workers or royalty touring the King's special project."

"But, why would she have been there? And how could she die and been buried without anyone knowing?" Dr Cooke asks.

"I don't know that," I admit. "But after she tested Solomon's knowledge and gave gifts to him, she isn't heard of again. But it is known that he was intrigued by her, and she him."

"But to have his child, and then to die, and be buried in the middle of a mine," the Professor shakes his head. "That would not be a Queen's final resting place, I can assure you."

"But it wasn't her final resting place," I remind him. "Half of her body is missing—she rests somewhere else, doesn't she?"

"Ugh," Griffin shivers. "All this talk about bones and missing bodies gives me the heebie-jeebies."

"Well, then you certainly wouldn't want to know that in order to bury noble people during the period, they first dehydrated the body, and then would use a metal instrument to pull out the organs through their nose and mouths and put them in jars," the Professor wiggles his eyebrows as Griffin gags.

"You're terrible, Albert," Dr Cooke chuckles.

"Right, so this woman—the Queen—you think that perhaps she has something to do with the ring?" Griffin swallows, trying to ignore the Professor.

"Well, her main reason for coming to Egypt was to test King Solomon's knowledge and theory of God. She was essentially there to draw him from his faith. But after a thorough test, King Solomon convinced her Jehovah existed," I say.

"Yes, but what does that have to do with the ring?" Griffin asks.

"The ring was given to King Solomon by God himself. It was inscribed with his name, and is meant to have great spiritual power. It's not a large leap to think that the woman whose sole purpose was to draw the King from his God, and then ended up being converted herself, would know something about the ring," I say, my eyes once again studying the papers around me. "It might not be with her, but she certainly has something to do with it."

"So, what are you saying? That we need to go to the mines where you saw the hieroglyphic? Do you think the ring might be down one of the mines?" Griffin asks.

"The mines have been searched, and so has the grave," Dr Cooke answers, shaking his head.

"Well, maybe it is in the ground somewhere, buried in the sand," Griffin suggests.

"The ring, if it exists," the Professor amends, "would be hidden in a very precise place. That is what these clues are for—that is, if they *are* actually clues."

"They are," I say firmly.

"Right, so now we just have to figure out where this

King's lost things are hidden. And no one else has been able to for what, two thousand years?" Griffin says, shaking his head.

"That's if our good friend Ahmed Gamal doesn't find it first," Dr Cooke qualifies. "Or discover we haven't left Egypt from our slippery friend, Thomas."

I try not to think about Thomas' involvement with Gamal. Quite frankly, I gave him a warning when I'm not even entirely sure he deserved one. I can't make him change his mind.

Still, I can't seem to get his wife's face from my mind. There was such pain as she stormed out of the Tanis exhibit and through the Tutankhamun–

Tutankhamun.

That's it.

"The ring is hidden," I say, looking at the horrible floral wallpaper behind the Professor's head.

"Yes, we know," the Professor mutters, picking up another picture.

"Where is the picture of the tomb?" I say, and start pushing papers aside as I look for the one I need.

"The tomb? The Tanis Pharaoh tomb?" Dr Cooke starts searching with me.

"It's here," the Professor says, pulling one of the file folders out of the pile.

"Did they do a thermal scan of the tomb?" I say, my eyes scanning the paperwork. I didn't bother to read when

I couldn't see the 'down' hieroglyphic anywhere in the picture, but now I realize the text is the key.

"I read that file," Dr Cooke says. "They haven't been able to get the equipment or a team there yet."

"Why does it matter?" Griffin asks, coming to stand over my shoulder to look at the papers.

"They *just* did a thermal scan on Tutankhamun's tomb—remember at the museum I told you they found hidden chambers in his tomb after performing a thermal scan?" I say, looking over my shoulder at him.

"So you think there could be a hidden chamber in the Tanis bloke's tomb?" Griffin asks, shaking his head. "If the ring is there though—what's the point of all of these bloody clues?"

"Because, it would be hidden, wouldn't it? Remember that when King Solomon's reign ended, which coincided with the United Monarch's reign, there was essentially a civil war in Egypt. All of the tombs along the Nile, and especially in the Valley of the Kings, were plundered," I explain.

"It does hold water," the Professor nods. "Think of the items that are missing from the King's treasure: the ark of the covenant, the golden table, the ring. All items that are invaluable and have *religious* significance. Perhaps they are missing for a reason."

"Someone took them and hid them, because they didn't want the plunderers to have items which essentially were divine," Dr Cooke nods. "The Knight's Templar found the ark and moved it themselves during the crusades. Perhaps they found the ring as well, but because of the rumoured power of it, they did not want to move or touch it. It falls in line that these items are something that the guardians do not want the unworthy to possess."

"Yes, but why the clues?" Griffin asks. "How do they know that we are worthy to find it?"

"Because plunderers don't take the time to search for things like this, follow clues," I explain. "They take what they can see in front of them and go to the next one."

"But if it's in some hidden chamber anyone who has one of those thermal camera things could find it," Griffin argues.

"Griffin, these people didn't have running water. They hunted for their food. They had no technology. They would not have even been able to fathom the *concept* of a thermal camera," I say. "They would have believed that only those who worked out the clues would have been able to find the treasure. And they weren't that wrong. People have searched using the Knight's Templar clues and no one has yet found the Holy Grail."

"So, you think it's in the tomb in some hidden compartment?" Griffin asks. "Even if we were able to get to the tomb it could take months—maybe years—to find any sort of hidden compartments."

"He's right, June," Dr Cooke says. "Tutankhamun's

tomb was discovered nearly one hundred years ago and they've only just come up with the theory of hidden rooms, and people have studied that tomb for years. Some of the tombs have hundreds of passageways."

"But, we *know* there is something in there. We know what to look for," I say.

"Still…" Dr Cooke hedges.

"Listen, we don't have the luxury of time, anyways," I say. "It is only a matter of time until Ahmed Gamal discovers we have found something out. I think we have one shot at this. We can go and look at the tomb, if it's not there, we pack it up, go home and scream to the world our theory in the hopes that somehow we might be sent back to excavate the tomb further."

"I like that," Griffin says. "Why don't we skip going to the tomb and get straight to the screaming bit?"

"Because I need to know we tried," I explain.

"We will need our armed guard, for all the use he is…" Dr Cooke says. "Though I'm not sure how kindly he will take to us rummaging around an old Egyptian tomb without permission."

"We will tell him very little until we get there," I say.

"And when we get there?" Griffin asks.

"We will do what we do best," I stand up. "Wing it."

A sudden knock at the door makes us all freeze.

I put my finger to my lips, looking at the others.

Dr Cooke nods in understanding.

I tip toe over to the door and look the peephole.

"Who is it?" the Professor whispers.

I sigh in relief.

"It's our faithful cameraman," I say, and open the door.

Clint stands on the other side of the door, twisting his hands together and not quite meeting my eyes.

"You're back," I say, raising my eyebrows in surprise.

He opens his mouth to reply but is cut off by the Professor's booming voice.

"Charlie, you're back!" he says, coming over to clap Clint on the back. "Just in time for the next adventure, jolly good."

"You've been missed, my boy!" Dr Cooke laughs, shaking his head and joining the Professor at the door. "Though we knew you would come to your senses. I was just saying that to you, wasn't I, Albert?"

"I believe I was the one who mentioned it," the Professor purses his lips and takes his journal out of his pocket.

"You bloody did not!" Dr Cooke says, pulling Clint into the suite and shutting the door before rounding on the Professor. "What are you writing in that journal? False information, it seems."

"You should know all about writing false information from that bloody bestselling novel of yours!" the Professor yells, pulling the journal to his chest.

"At least people want to read what *I* write," Dr Cooke

shoots back, red splotches forming on his cheeks.

"You keep telling yourself that," the Professor says, patting him on the shoulder.

"The cheek! Clint, I need you in my room in five minutes. You can help me answer my fan mail," Dr Cooke says, storming out of the room.

"Has your dentist been writing again, then?" the Professor yells, following Dr Cooke into the other room.

I blink at the now empty doorway the two of them disappeared through before turning to Clint, who looks flabbergasted at the scene.

"So you're back?" I ask him again.

"Er–" Clint frowns, thinking for a moment.

"Of course he is." Griffin, claps him on the back, nodding his head. "Knew you'd do the right thing, mate."

Griffin shakes Clint's hand before walking into our bedroom.

Clint looks down at his hand and looks very pleased with Griffin's statement.

"What did you really come back for?" I ask him, trying to hide amusement.

Clint looks up at me for a moment, obviously deciding how to answer.

"You have my passport in your bag," he admits.

I smile.

Chapter Eighteen

"They said they would be right back," I mutter, peering over Griffin's shoulder. "What could possibly be taking them so long?"

"June you've put the two worst people for the task," Griffin shakes his head. "The wind keeps blowing the sand in my eye."

"Well, I thought maybe Clint would be able to steer them in the right direction, considering he's got some things to make up for," I say. "And I had to sort this out."

I hold up the file folder, which Griffin eyes with apprehension.

"You think it will work?" he asks.

"If Simon wants this story bad enough, it had better," I say. "Oh, here they are now."

I spy the Professor first as he rounds the tall rock's edge, holding a rope.

"Got them June!" he yells. Griffin and I immediately tell him to be quiet.

"Sorry!"

"Oh, good God," Griffin mutters and slowly closes his

eyes as Dr Cooke, Clint, and Omar round the corner as well.

"Aren't they magnificent?" the Professor beams.

"What—you were supposed to get *horses*," I say, throwing my arms into the air.

"Well they only had one left and I wanted us all to match," the Professor says, stroking the neck of a rather dishevelled looking camel.

"But we need to get there *quickly*," I argue, looking up to the sky at the setting sun.

"They are quite quick," Dr Cooke laughs. "Clint now knows to keep a rather tight grip on his. It's why we took so long, couldn't catch it."

"June, it was magnificent," the Professor chuckles, wiping his eyes.

"Yes, well we are all here now," Clint says, rolling his eyes at them. "Can we just get on with it?"

"You've only got three," I say.

"It's all they had left, but the man said they are strong and we can double up," Dr Cooke explains.

"This is true Ms Jenson. They can easily carry two of us with your bags," Omar confirms.

I briefly smile and nod, but then look away. I've noticed Omar looking at me a lot recently. I mean, I'm sure he is very curious as to what we are doing here, in the entrance to the Valley of the Kings so late at night with equipment. But the great thing about Omar is he doesn't ask many questions. I can see they are there, on the tip of his tongue, but he doesn't ask them.

Or maybe the Professor has promised that I will marry him. It really wouldn't surprise me at this point.

"Right, well we can double up then," I say turning to Griffin.

"Clint you go with the Professor and Dr Cooke can travel with Omar in the lead. You said you knew the way to the Tanis Pharaoh's tomb, correct?" Griffin asks.

Omar nods.

"Right, Clarence, you'll have to give me a bit of a boost then," the Professor says, pointing to the camel.

"How am I meant to get on, then?" Clint shakes his head.

"You're younger and much more flexible," the Professor explains. "You can just jump up."

"His back is eight feet off the ground!" Clint looks up at the shifting torso of the camel.

"Do you sit on the humps or in between them?" Dr Cooke asks, tilting his head.

"I'll help everyone get on and then Griffin can pull me up," I volunteer.

It takes a great deal of grunting on my part, but I eventually have everyone situated on a camel with our extra backpacks and equipment.

I walk over to Griffin's outstretched hand and my feet leave the ground as he pulls me in front of him on the camel.

"Right, lead the way," I say to Omar.

Travelling by camel is actually quite tricky. They are constantly lurching forwards and backwards and my body soon becomes fatigued with the effort of centring my balance.

After twenty minutes I feel Griffin shiver from behind me.

"It's absolutely freezing here," Griffin says, wrapping his arms more tightly around me.

"That's a tricky part of the Valley of the Kings and what actually kept a lot of the tombs protected from looters," I explain. "Because of the rock valleys and desert climate it is stifling hot during the day, but the temperatures plummet in the evening. It was too cold for many to brave it to plunder the tombs—especially when they didn't know if there was anything to find there."

"Don't be afraid to get close, Craig," the Professor says, snuggling closer to Clint. "The body warmth with do us both good."

I smile widely.

"Omar, your aftershave, is that a hint of jasmine I detect?" Dr Cooke asks, his face tilted in the crook of Omar's neck.

"Are there not going to be guards at the tombs?" Clint asks, trying to put a few inches between him and the Professor.

"That's why we got Simon to get the government to issue an ordinance, giving us permission to take some night time pictures of the tomb," I say, pointing to my knapsack where the paperwork rests.

"Will they fall for it?" Griffin asks in my ear, careful to not let his voice carry to Omar.

"It was good enough to fool me when I first saw it," I say, shrugging. "Though I can't really read Arabic. I was only able to garner the gist. But the seals and signatures looked authentic. I guess we will have to wait and see."

We continue on for another half hour, passing many tomb openings along the way, all of which are sealed with heavy metal gates with padlocks. I look forward and tell myself for what seems like the hundredth time that Omar said he knew where he is going.

"It isn't much further," Omar yells over his shoulder.

I let out a sigh of relief, but it catches almost immediately as a small truck approaches us from the North.

"Clint, it might be time to get out your camera," I suggest quickly.

Clint roots in his bag and pulls out his camera.

"What shall I film?" he asks.

"The different tomb openings," I say, and have to raise my voice for him to hear me over the loud motor of the approaching car.

I feel the camel shift sideways in a nervous gesture at the growing sound.

The army green truck with no roof is upon is in seconds, and I am suddenly looking down the barrel of a semi-automatic weapon.

"You are trespassing," the soldier says, his commanding voice making me shrink.

"Er—hello there!" I say, adopting a friendly smile. "My name is June Jenson, and I—"

"You do not have permission to be here," the soldier says, cutting me off. "Turn around and leave at once or you will be arrested."

"You don't have to ask me twice," the Professor says, and starts to turn the camel's head with the reins.

"Ms Jenson, if you will allow me," Omar says, putting his hand on his heart.

Startled, I just nod.

Omar begins a rapid conversation with the soldier, and I find my head moving between the two of them, trying to determine what is being said even though my Arabic is beyond rusty. Something I am determined to rectify the minute I get home. If we make it home.

"Ms Jenson, you said you have paperwork?" Omar says, holding out his hand.

"Oh—er, yes of course," I say, reaching round and pulling the paperwork out of my knapsack.

Thinking better of trying to coax the camel over to Omar, I quickly slide off and run over to hand it to him.

Omar effortlessly turns his own camel and trots over to

the soldier.

Dr Cooke's eyes are wide with fright as he clings to Omar's middle.

The soldier takes the paperwork from Omar's outstretched hand and scans it. I hold my breath.

Oh god, I should have translated exactly what the paperwork said before we left. What if the soldier questions me about it? About some sort of specific wording in there.

My palms are dripping with sweat despite the frigid temperatures.

The soldier finally finishes the document and slowly looks up.

"You are a television star?" he asks, looking me up and down in disbelief.

Alright, well he's not catching me quite at my best. I mean, usually I am not wearing two sweaters, and I typically wear *some* makeup.

"Yes," I say, raising my chin.

He drums his fingers on the side of the truck as he stares at me.

I stare back at him, determined to not cower.

"You will be gone by morning?" he asks.

"Yes, of course. We are only interested in filming at night for this segment," I explain.

He looks down at the paperwork once more before folding it and tucking it into his pocket.

"You will follow me," he says, climbing back into the driver's seat of his truck.

He starts the engine and quickly turns the truck around, which is quite impressive in the narrow lane of sand between the valley rocks.

"June," Griffin says, having walked the camel over. He reaches his hand out to me. "Come on."

I shake my head for a moment to clear it and then nod. Reaching up, Griffin pulls me back onto the camel and we follow after Omar and Dr Cooke.

"Where is he taking us?" I whisper to Griffin.

"I don't know," he says. "But I think it's a bit useless to run now. He'd catch us in less than a minute with that truck."

My hands shake as I stare at the back of Dr Cooke. I can only imagine how terrified he is, his arms tightly wrapped around Omar's middle.

I look over my shoulder to see the Professor following behind us. We meet eyes and he nods once at me.

We travel for another quarter of an hour before the truck suddenly stops and the soldier climbs out.

"This is the Tanis tomb," he says, pointing to his left. "I will unlock the gates. You will touch nothing inside."

Dr Cooke's eyes widen as he nods his head frantically.

"I patrol this mile of the valley," the soldier says. "I will check back. You will touch nothing inside."

"Yes, we got that," Griffin says from behind me.

The soldier turns his gaze to Griffin and pauses.

I elbow Griffin telling him to remain quiet.

"You will be gone by the morning. And you will touch nothing inside."

I sense Griffin nod behind me.

The soldier stares at me for a moment.

"I did not know the Minister of Sport had a British niece," the soldier says.

My eyes widen a fraction before I am able to control the reaction.

Terrified to say anything, I just smile.

He studies me for a moment more before walking over to the tall wrought iron gates that seal off the entrance to the tomb.

He pulls a ring of keys out of his pocket and after he finds the right one he turns to the lock and opens the door.

"I will be back," he says, closing the truck door and starting the engine. "And you will touch nothing inside."

His tires kick up sand and we watch him disappear into the distance.

"You know, I suddenly have the urge to touch something," Griffin says, sliding off the camel behind me.

The rest of us carefully make our way off the camels and tie their reins to a metal hook protruding from a nearby rock. Walking over to the sand covered steps that lead down into the tomb I take note of the heavy wrought iron gates.

"Now might be a good time to mention I get a little claustrophobic," Clint swallows, looking into the black entrance.

I fish in my knapsack for the flashlight and turn it on. The narrow beam of light barely produces a faint glow in the darkness. I hear multiple clicks and look around to see the others have followed suit.

"Would you like to stay out here with Omar?" I ask Clint, taking note of his shaking beam of light.

"Er–" Clint looks over to Omar and shakes his head. "No, I'll stay with you."

"Well, let's go see what we can find, shall we?"

Chapter Nineteen

After twenty or so steps we reach flat ground in a rectangular shaped chamber.

I direct my light along the wall closest to me and my breath catches at the intricate artwork on the wall.

"It's breath-taking, isn't it?" Dr Cooke asks, coming to stand beside me, removing his hat.

"Stunning," I agree, my eyes roaming the wall, trying to take in all of the detail of the pictures.

"Did they paint this?" Griffin asks, coming to stand on my other side.

Clint removes his camera from his bag and begins to film as we shine the light.

"They are called reliefs," I explain. "See how the stone has been first carved to make the figures stand out from the surface? They first carved the stones, and then layered plaster on top to smooth out their work before painting."

"It's amazing," Griffin shakes his head. "That they had this sort of talent with the basic knowledge of materials. To think this is what people spent their time and talent on, when now a days most people's leisure time is spent in front of the telly."

"How did they paint it?" Clint asks, walking closer with his camera.

"Whatever local supplies they could find," the Professor explains, his face a foot away from the wall as he studies the work. "They used a primitive version of chalk lines to ensure the proportions were right.

The Professor raises his finger to show the camera.

"A lot of the pigments they used to create paint were local, though some unusual colours derived from foreign materials which help us track trade alliances," he explains. "This black would be carbon, the yellow and reds iron, the gold is orpiment. They would grind into a powder and mix with a plant based glue."

I step back and wave my light throughout the rest of the room.

"There are four burial beds in here," I say, shining my light on each one.

"Was this where King Solomon was buried?" Griffin asks, training his own light next to mine to create a brighter glow.

"No, this is only the antechamber," I explain. "This would be were his wives or children were buried."

"There are hundreds of bodies in this tomb, then?" Griffin asks, and suddenly takes a tentative step back.

"No, just a select few. Others would be buried elsewhere. Many of them were spread all over Egypt," I say, taking a step closer to the rock beds where the sarcophaguses once rested.

"Do you think the hidden chamber would be here?" Clint asks, scanning the walls again.

I shake my head.

"I think if it is here it would be off the treasury room, or the King's burial chamber," I say, and turn to the Professor for confirmation.

"Yes, I believe you're right," the Professor says, wiping his brow with his handkerchief.

"Well, we better get at it," Griffin says, coming to stand beside me. "I'm not sure how much time we have before G.I. Joe comes back."

"Right," I nod and raise the beam of light to the left side of the chamber. "That tunnel leads to the annex."

I turn my light to the right side.

"So this is where we need to go to access the burial chamber. The treasury is off of that," I say.

"Ladies first," Clint says, his camera shaking in his hands.

I roll my eyes and walk towards the narrow passageway.

Another fifty paces or so and we enter another, much smaller chamber.

"That is where his sarcophagus lay," I say, pointing to the rock platform in the middle of the room. "His organs were in jars in a chest which wasn't on display in Cairo, they decided to showcase the funeral bowls instead.

I peer around the room, but there isn't much to it

besides stone walls and a few sunken reliefs.

"Well, it doesn't look like it is hidden in anything in here," Griffin says. "There's nothing here."

"Hmm," I nod, and go over to the other doorway and walk through.

The treasury is cleared out as well.

Griffin appears beside me.

"They clear everything out due to current day grave robbers," I tell him. "The government only open a few tombs to tourists at a time and will bring artefacts back to display and then return them to carefully monitored storage facilities when they aren't on display at the museum."

"So you think there could be something hidden behind the walls?" Griffin asks, running his hand over the rough edges of the stone wall to his right. "How would we know?"

"I'm not sure," I say, shaking my head. "Let's go back to the burial chamber and start there."

Griffin and I re-enter the burial chamber to see Dr Cooke and the Professor shining their lights on the reliefs.

"We thought we might get a clue from these," Dr Cooke explains, squinting his eyes. "But it's hard to see in this light."

"We brought a flood light," I say, taking off my knapsack and walking over to the Professor. "I could set it up in the corner there and we could get better lighting in here. It's back with Omar and the camels."

"I'll go and get it," the Professor suggests.

"Er—I think you better stay here," I say to him, not sure I want him wandering around the tomb by himself. "I'll go."

"No, I'll go," Clint says, handing me his camera. "I think I might need a bit of air, anyways."

"You know how to get back?" I ask him.

"Yes, I think so," he nods. "Though if I'm not back in ten minutes feel free to send out a search party."

I nod and he turns and walks back through to the passageway to the antechamber.

"So what picture are we looking for?" Griffin frowns as he studies the wall in front of him. "The one for up or the one for down?"

"Both," I shrug. "I'll start over here."

I begin to read the hieroglyphics in front of me but they mainly speak of Osiris, which isn't surprising, as he was the Egyptian God of death.

"Up, down; maybe we are supposed to be looking for another direction," Dr Cooke suggests, studying the wall in front of him. "If they were the clues in other places, they aren't likely to be the clues in here, are they?"

"Maybe they are a sort of map to navigate where we are supposed to look in the tomb," Griffin suggests, turning to face us. "We're lower here right? So maybe up is the entrance, and down is the furthest part in the treasury."

"Yes, but there was no clue between the two, was

there?" the Professor asks. "It would not be that broad, it would be a very specific place."

"And there was nothing on the tomb? No other picture?" Griffin asks, looking at me.

No, just the arrow," I say, biting my bottom lip.

Dr Cooke is right. We are missing a clue after 'down'. There must be something more specific to detail the location of the ring. But there was only the arrow.

The arrow.

My hand moves the light away from the wall while my brain sprints to catch up with my train of thought.

"The arrow," I say. "It points the seeker in a direction."

"Yes," Dr Cooke says, frowning at me.

Without explaining I raise my light to the ceiling.

"Up," I mutter.

The ceiling is solid with light swirls of sand dust collecting in the light's beam.

"Down," I whisper, and move the light until it catches the stone base in the middle of the burial chamber.

There's a loud bang in the distance behind me.

"Clint's probably fallen down the bloody stairs," Griffin shakes his head and takes a step towards the passageway.

"The arrow," I repeat in wonderment. "I know where the ring is!"

I turn around, and quickly walk over to the entrance

way.

"June, where are you going?" Dr Cooke asks.

"I need the light!" Just as I enter the passageway I'm blinded by a bright light.

"Clint! I can't see anything," I argue, bringing my hands up to block out the light and taking a step backwards.

The light is lowered and my eyes take a moment to stop seeing bright halos.

I finally blink my surroundings back into focus, and inhale.

Omar stands before me, his long slender finger wrapped around the trigger of a gun that is pointed at me.

Chapter Twenty

"Omar?" I frown, and take a step backwards.

"I want the ring, Ms Jenson," Omar says, walking towards me.

"What in the blazes?" Dr Cooke says, looking from Omar to me. "Put that down at once!"

"I'm sorry, my friend, but I cannot," Omar says, not taking his eyes off of me. "I need the ring."

"Where is Clint?" I ask, quickly looking over Omar's shoulder.

"He is in the antechamber, he took a rather nasty blow to the head, I'm afraid," Omar says without the slightest hint of regret in his tone.

"You bastard!" the Professor yells. "We trusted you!"

"I heard you—you just said you knew where the ring is," Omar states, ignoring the Professor's outburst. "I want it. Give it to me."

"I—how did you know we were looking for the ring?" I ask.

"Your grandfather told me the first day you arrived, while I was putting the luggage in the van," he says.

I turn to the Professor, whose eyes are wide.

"Er—" he purses his lips. "I might have mentioned something…"

"But, I don't understand," I say, shaking my head. "You've never said anything. You were going to let us go to the airport."

"Mr Gamal said you gave him the clue," Omar says. "That you were allowed to leave."

"You work for Ahmed Gamal?" I ask in a strangled voice.

"My family, like so many in Cairo, owes Ahmed Gamal a lot of money," Omar explains. "When your friend Thomas told Mr. Gamal's men you were looking for the ring, Gamal discovered I was your translator. He knew I would be able to tell him where you were staying and told me he would forgive my debt if I gave him any useful information on your whereabouts."

"You were the one who led him to the hotel," I say, my eyes never wavering from his face. Or from the gun still pointing at my chest.

"Yes, but you escaped them, and got in my van," Omar says, smiling. "You are very resourceful, Ms Jenson."

"Why didn't you tell him where we were going after that?" Griffin interjects from across the room.

Omar turns his head slightly, but the gun doesn't move.

"I was about to drive you to his house myself, but I heard you in the car telling the others you had solved a clue about the ring's location," Omar says, returning his attention to me. "I decided on a better course of action."

"You decided to follow me, and if I found the ring you would keep it for yourself," I say.

Omar shakes his head.

"No, Ms Jenson. I have no use for that ring," Omar smiles.

"I don't understand," I frown.

"How much greater will I be rewarded when I present the ring to Gamal, when I and I alone was able to procure it?" Omar asks. "He will forgive my debt and reward me ten fold. Ahmed Gamal is the best ally you could ever dream to have in Egypt."

"So he doesn't know we are here?" I ask.

"No, he believes I am taking you to the airport as I told him I was," Omar says.

"Aren't you worried your boss will find out you lied?" Griffin asks, taking a further step towards me. He's covered half the distance between us.

"He went to Timna with your reporter friend," Omar explains. "Tell me where the ring is, Ms Jenson."

Omar points the gun at my head, tilting his head to the side.

Griffin takes another step towards me, and Omar pulls back the safety.

"Not another step, my friend," Omar warns Griffin. "Don't make me ask again, Ms Jenson."

"And if I refuse?" I say, lifting my eyebrow and displaying a sense of coolness that I certainly do not feel.

"I will shoot you," Omar says in a matter-of-fact tone.

"If you shoot me you will never know where the ring is," I tell him.

I can feel Griffin slowly, an inch at a time, drawing ever so closer to me. I put my hand out to the side to try and tell him to stop—to stay away—but he either does not see it, or chooses to ignore it.

"Where is the ring, Ms Jenson?" Omar asks again, taking a step towards me.

"I—I don't know," I say, defiantly lifting my chin.

"You refuse to tell me, although it might mean your death?" he asks, tilting his head to the side.

I stare at Omar, refusing to show him how afraid I am.

"I will give you to the count of five," Omar explains.

"June!" Griffin says, holding his hands up to Omar. "For Christ's sake, just tell him where the bloody ring is."

"No," I say, pushing the bridge of my glasses further up my nose. "I would rather die than have the ring be handed over to someone like Ahmed Gamal."

"You care more about history than your own life?" he asks, frowning slightly.

"We all have something we believe in," I say to him. "I've met people like you my whole life. People who profit off the history that has shaped our world. You don't care about what this could mean to the people of Egypt, you care about money and lining your pocket! Well, I'm sick of it. And I won't ever tell you where that ring is, so you can just go and tell your boss or whoever he is that there's something his money cannot buy in this world. And it's *me.*"

"Interesting," he says, nodding. "But there is something you care more about then history, I am sure."

I narrow my eyes as Omar starts to smile.

I put my hand out to stop him but it's not my scream that meets the sounds of the gun going off.

"No!" I hear Dr Cooke scream and see a blur as he jumps in front of the Professor.

In a moment that seems like it lasts for an eternity Dr Cooke is suspended in air before he crashes to the ground.

"Daniel!" the Professor cries, falling to his knees in front of Dr Cooke. "No! No!"

"Albert," Dr Cooke's hand, now covered in blood from the wound in his stomach, shakes as it reaches for the Professor.

"You bastard!" I yell, lunging for Omar, but Griffin grabs me around the stomach and holds me back as Omar once again has the gun pointed to me, the smile still on his face.

The tears pour down my cheeks as I look away from his face to where the Professor is kneeling beside Dr Cooke.

I pull myself away from Griffin and run over to them.

"Dr Cooke," I sob through the tears, taking his handkerchief out of his pocket and applying it to the wound. I slip the bunched up fabric under his belt to hold the pressure. "I'm so sorry. God, I'm so sorry."

"You bloody fool," the Professor says to Dr Cooke, silent tears spilling down his face.

"Albert," Dr Cooke looks weakly up at the Professor and smiles. "My friend. It has… been an honour."

Dr Cooke's words are laboured and the Professor shakes his head.

"Save your strength," the Professor says, clutching Dr Cooke's hand. "We will get you out of here. We will get you home."

"Home," Dr Cooke sighs, looking from me to the Professor. "You two were the only home I've ever needed."

Dr Cooke turns his white face to Griffin who kneels down beside me.

"Look after my family," Dr Cooke tells him.

I see Griffin nod once beside me. He wraps his arm around my shaking shoulders.

Dr Cooke lifts his head a fraction to look down at the handkerchief and his own blood stained hand.

He lets out a final sigh and closes his eyes, his body going limp.

"No!" I sob, my hand grasping Dr Cooke's arm.

The Professor sits back on the ground, holding his

head between his hands.

"I hate to break up the funeral," Omar says from behind me, "but we really do need to find the ring."

Griffin stands up quickly from besides me and makes to lunge at Omar.

"I don't think so," Omar says, raising his gun higher. "Unless Ms Jenson wants more blood on her hands."

"You killed him," I spit out, still kneeling by Dr Cooke's lifeless body. "You killed an innocent man!"

"And I'm willing to kill the rest of them to get what I want," Omar says, looking at me. "Shall I kill your grandfather next, or perhaps your lover?"

The tears stream down my face as I stare at the calm look on Omar's features.

He killed Dr Cooke. He will kill the rest of my family. And it will be all my fault.

No piece of history is worth that. It was naive and stupid of me to not realize that sooner. And my pride cost Dr Cooke his life.

I won't let him kill anyone else I love.

"It's under the burial platform," I say, pointing to the stone in the middle of the chamber.

Chapter Twenty-One

"Below the platform?" Omar asks. "How can you be sure?"

I wipe the wet streaks from my cheek as I stare at him in pure loathing.

"Does it matter? I say, my face full of hatred. "That's where your treasure is. Take it and leave my family alone."

Omar shakes his head.

"Explain or they die as well," he warns.

I pause, trying to get a hold on my rage.

"The hieroglyphics were two-fold clues," I explain. "They were first intended to direct the seeker to the location of the ring, the petroglyph leading us 'up' the Nile, and the 'down' hieroglyphic leading us to Luxor, the Valley of the Kings."

Omar looks down, studying the ground by the platform, before returning my gaze. "And the second part?"

"The hieroglyphic was also on the grave site with the arrow to explain that the symbols were also more simplistic directions, up," I say, pointing my finger to the ceiling and then lowering it, "and down."

"What is in the ceiling?" Omar says, looking up.

"Nothing," I shake my head.

"I don't understand," he frowns.

"It is not *up* from our perspective, but from *hers*," I explain.

"Who?" Omar asks, looking at Griffin and then to the Professor, who still clings to Dr Cooke's body.

"The Queen of Sheba," I say. "The arrow was found at her gravesite, or what was originally her gravesite."

"The Queen of Sheba?" Omar asks. "The woman who was sent to test King Solomon's faith?"

"She was the lover no one knew the King had," I say. "If the Egyptians knew who she was—of who they were burying—they never would have left her in that hole. She would have been given a proper burial. But someone found out. The same person who took the ring, and buried it below King Solomon."

"But, why was half of her body left in the makeshift grave?" Griffin asks, and I can see he uses the question to get closer to me again as the gun is still trained on my chest.

"Because they needed to in order to lead the seeker here," I explain pointing to the burial rock. "She now rests below her lover, with his greatest possession."

"Up and down," Griffin nods. "She is below him and he is above."

"You are a very clever woman," Omar says, nodding. "Now get up."

My jaw clenches at the command, but I get to my feet.

"You know where the ring is," I say, pushing my glasses up the bridge of my nose. "Now let my family go."

"I don't think so," he laughs. "Not until I have the ring, my friend."

"How do I know you won't just kill us anyways after we give it to you?" I ask.

"You don't," he shrugs. "Now move the rock."

I study his unwavering expression and clench my teeth as my chin shakes.

"How are we going to move that bloody heavy rock?" Griffin asks him, his own rage bubbling just below the surface.

"Figure it out," Omar enunciates each word, turning the gun on Griffin.

I scan the room and my eye stops on one of the unlit torches.

"We can use these," I say, walking over to the thick pieces of wood. "We can use them as levers and distribute the weight."

"Will that work?" Griffin asks, his eyes darting from me to the gun.

"It's the best chance we have," I say.

I walk over to the Professor and touch his shoulder which causes him to jump.

"Professor," I say, my voice choked. "We need your help."

The Professor looks up at me, frowning.

"Help? I don't think I have time," he says, shaking his head as his head twitches to the side. "I have a meeting, I have a…"

His voice trails off and he begins to rock back and forth again.

"I'm so sorry," I say, trying to contain my sob. "If you help us, I will get you to your meeting, I promise."

"My meeting?" the Professor says, looking around the chamber. "Where is my meeting?"

"I will take you," I say, taking the Professor's hands off Dr Cooke and pulling him to his feet. "I will take you, if you could just help us for a moment."

The Professor blinks at me, and shakes his head.

"I'm not sure I can," he whispers.

"I'll show you," I say, squeezing his hands. "I'll show you how."

I lead the Professor over to the burial stone, not taking my eyes off of him.

"Here, I got more from the treasury," Griffin says, and hands both the Professor and me a torch.

"I have a meeting," the Professor frowns at Griffin.

Griffin smiles kindly and squeezes the Professor's shoulder.

"I know, we'll get you there," he promises.

"The platform is raised a few inches from the ground," I say, pointing to the bottom. "The recessed rock must be the opening for the underground chamber that the burial rock is sitting on. If we put our torches underneath the rock and put our weight on the other end, it will hopefully be enough to move the top stone."

"And if it's not?" Griffin asks.

I shake my head.

"It's the best chance we have," I whisper.

I wedge the wooden staff under the side of the rock and pull the Professor's arm.

"You take this one Professor," I say.

When Griffin and I have our torches wedged I nod.

"Alright on three," I say. "One, two, three!"

On three I put all my weight on the staff and the others follow suit. For a moment I think it didn't work, but then my body lowers further as the counterbalance lifts the stone from its base.

"Right," I pant once the staffs are parallel to the ground. "Now everyone push down while pulling the staff towards them. It will shift the rock to the side of the opening. Now!"

With a great grunt I put my weight once again on the staff and then pull it towards me. The rock lurches to the side and I fall backwards from the momentum.

Griffin's hands are on my arms and he pulls me up to my feet. I look down and see there is an opening just big enough for someone to fit through.

I'm momentarily stunned at the sight. I was right, there

is a hidden chamber below.

"Well?" Omar says, the gun still pointed at me. "What's down there?"

I pick up my flashlight from beside my knapsack on the ground where I left it, and walk over to the opening.

I crouch down on my knees and shine the beam down the dark hole.

"There is definitely another chamber down there," I nod. "The bottom is about fifteen feet below."

"We would break our legs with that kind of a fall," Griffin says, shaking his head.

"You go first and we will see if your assessment is accurate," Omar says, smiling.

"There is a ladder," I say, reaching my hand into the darkness to encounter the first wooden rung.

"Well, Ms Jenson," Omar takes a step closer. "I believe the custom is ladies first."

"I'll go first," Griffin volunteers, stepping in front of me.

"No, I don't think so," Omar says, shaking his head. "Ms Jenson will go first, followed by myself. If you and her dear grandfather don't follow us, well, I'll let you conclude what will happen to Ms Jenson."

I put my hand on Griffin's arm.

"I'll be fine," I whisper.

"You are wasting valuable time," Omar says. "Move!"

I walk around Griffin's stiff form and turn around at

the floor chamber's opening.

"Make sure you put your feet by the outer edges of the ladder," I tell Griffin and the Professor. "The wood may not be strong after all of this time."

Griffin nods.

I lean over the opening and drop my flashlight; it hits the floor below and rolls to the side.

"That will help you see where the bottom is," I tell the Professor, but I am not sure he can even hear me speaking.

I put my first foot in the hole, my hands balancing my weight on the stone opening. My other foot joins and then lowers to find the second rung. On the third, with just my head above ground I look at Griffin.

"Look after him," I whisper.

Griffin's jaw tightens and he nods.

"I'll be right behind, I promise," he says.

Without another word I find the next rung and slowly lower myself down into the chamber.

"Both of you on the far wall until I am down!" I hear Omar yell. "If you come before I beckon you I will shoot her in the head."

I don't hear the response as my feet finally touch the ground. Wiping my hands down the front of my trousers I quickly scan the room, but it is impossible to see anything.

Omar is half way down the ladder when he stops and points the gun that is still in his one hand at me.

"Back up, Ms Jenson," he commands.

I do what I am told and watch as he makes his way to the ground. He quickly looks around after turning his own flashlight on, but it doesn't make much of a dent in the darkness.

"Come down now!" he yells to the chamber above us. "And bring the floodlight."

I watch as the Professor begins to climb down, his hands trembling while mumbling to himself. The words are incoherent and my heart breaks.

I did this to him. I am responsible for this, for Dr Cooke. The thought of Dr Cooke brings fresh tears that pour down my cheeks and I bring my hand to my trembling mouth. There is no way I can fix it. I can't make it right. I can't bring him back, and it is something I will never forgive myself for. I just pray to God I am able to get the Professor and Griffin out of this alive. I *have* to get them out of here safely.

The Professor reaches the ground and starts pacing back and forth, a few feet in each direction. I walk over to him and wrap my arm around him. He flinches.

"Stay with me, Professor," I say to him softly. "I'll take care of you."

"I have a meeting." He looks at me in confusion.

"That's right, I'll take you," I say, stroking his arm.

I look up at the sound of Griffin making his way down the ladder, awkwardly trying to hold onto the rung with one hand and the handle for the portable floodlight with the other.

When he finally reaches the ground he walks over to me.

"I'm alright," I assure him.

"Turn on the light," Omar orders, the whites of his eyes just visible in the darkness.

Griffin reaches down to press the button.

Light shines to every corner of the room and once again my eyes take a moment to adjust to the sudden brightness.

When I finally look up, I gasp. The walls of the chamber are lined with more treasure then I have ever seen in one place; the tarnished gold still glistening under the floodlight's glare. Sculptures, tapestries, and piles of gold coins fill every corner of the chamber.

"It's the lost treasure of King Solomon," I breathe.

My eyes dart from one piece to the next, trying to take it all in.

A solid gold statue beside me of a woman holding out her hands. Her outstretched hands hold precious gemstones and gold nuggets.

The rug she rests on is worn almost to the point of ruin under her feet from years of deterioration. My eyes lift and focus on the centre of the room where a sarcophagus lies.

"It is true," Omar whispers in disbelief, his eyes also fixed on the sarcophagus. "But where is the ring?"

He turns to me again with the gun.

"It will be with her," I say, nodding to the middle of the room.

"Open it," Omar commands.

"I—I might damage the sarcophagus," I argue. "There is hundreds of years of history here."

"Open it," Omar slowly repeats.

I look at the Professor whose eyes are wide as he closely examines a solid gold urn embossed with jewels.

I swallow and nod.

"I need your help," I say to Griffin.

Together we walk over to the sarcophagus. What I thought was made of a dark coloured pottery, I realize is actually solid silver which has greatly tarnished over the years.

"It will be very heavy," I say to Griffin, running my fingers along the edge to find the seam. "Take a deep breath and hold it, do not breath in until you are as far away from this as possible—I'm not sure what sort of state she will be in or what the embalming materials will be like."

Griffin looks panicked but nods once.

"What's the plan, June?" Griffin says in such a low whisper I barely hear. I look up and Omar is watching us, but I don't think he heard Griffin.

"I don't know," I breathe back as I lean over to examine the sarcophagus and hide my lips from Omar. "But I am not losing anyone else today."

An image of Dr Cooke flashes through my mind but I

push it away and swallow the lump in my throat. There will be time for grief later. I have the rest of my life to relive the mistakes I've made. But I won't let that grief take Griffin or the Professor right now.

"I think there's an edge here," I say, loud enough for Omar to hear.

Griffin bends slightly on the pretence of looking at it.

"When we take this lid off get him over here to see the ring," Griffin whispers.

"Why? What are you going to do?" I ask, my eyes widening at the thought of Griffin playing the hero and getting shot.

He shakes his head once and stands up straighter.

Standing side-by-side we each put our fingers in the groove.

"Deep breath on two, lift on three," I command. "One, two, three."

I take a deep breath and lift with all my might as the lid lifts and falls away to the side.

I cover my mouth instinctively but when I look down I slowly let out my breath.

The bones, arranged so deliberately, are covered in cobwebs and dust, but there is nothing protecting them. The hands that rest beside where her stomach would have been appear to be cupping a small golden box.

I look up at Omar whose eyes are wide with delight, and I think a little fear.

"It's in the box," I say, pointing.

"Pick it up," he commands.

"I—I can't," I say, shaking head and I feel Griffin step away. "It is said to control demons to the one who possesses it. I can't—"

Suddenly there is a loud bang as the gun in Omar's hand goes off and my heart seems to stop. Looking up, I frown as Omar stumbles to the side, dropping the weapon to the ground.

The Professor stands holding a large urn that he must have struck Omar's arm with. The Professor raises it again as Omar lunges for the gun on the ground.

Griffin catches Omar around the middle and tackles him to the ground. As the two struggle, pieces of the treasure begin to get knocked over and fall to the ground.

Griffin grunts as Omar's fist connects with his jaw, but Griffin's hand maintains its grip on Omar' throat.

There is suddenly another large bang and I jump as I see the Professor holding the gun to the ceiling and then levelling it at Omar.

"Get up," the Professor commands, his hand no longer trembling.

Griffin stills and promptly gets off Omar. He keeps his gaze on the Professor.

I look down and see the little gold box in the tomb. Without thinking about it, I reach in and pull the box out. It is much lighter than I thought it would be. My fingers wipe away the dust from the top of the box and grip it, pulling the two pieces apart.

There, inside, is the golden ring that once belonged to God himself. The shank is wide and thick, but surprisingly small. The shoulders are laden with three stones each, the centre is a solid blue emerald. When I turn the box, for a moment I think I see something inside of the stone, but then the reflection moves and it disappears.

"Is it the ring?" Griffin asks, staring at me.

Careful not to touch the ring, I cover it with the lid once more. I look up at Griffin and blink, then turn my attention to the Professor.

Chapter Twenty-Two

The Professor keeps the gun pointed on Omar and I can see his face trembling with anger. I walk over to him and gently put my hand on his arm.

He jumps slightly at my touch, but doesn't take his eyes from Omar's.

"He killed Daniel," the Professor says, his voice shaking.

"I know," I say, my voice trembling with my own emotion.

"He deserves to die," he says, meeting my eyes for a moment.

"Perhaps," I say, looking into his pain filled blue eyes. "But you don't deserve to be a killer. You're the better man."

He studies me, his eyes filled with tears, before he exhales and lowers his arm.

"What are we going to do with him?" Griffin asks, taking the gun from the Professor.

"We are going to turn him into the Egyptian authorities and tell them about our discovery so it can be properly documented and removed," I say to them both. "Then afterwards maybe we can tell Ahmed Gamal where he is, and he can come and collect his debt himself."

Omar whimpers in front me.

"Except for this," I say, holding the box containing the ring for him to see. "We will hold onto this piece until we reach the British embassy—just in case the Egyptian government sees things more in Mr. Gamal's favour. It is the last discovery made by Dr Daniel Cooke."

"You are just going to leave me here?" Omar says, his eyes darting around the dark chamber.

"We'll make sure you are found, but I think we'll wait until we are safely on the plane to England," I say. "Give you some time to sit here and think about what's to come."

The Professor and Griffin follow me over to the ladder, Griffin keeping the gun pointed on Omar's kneeling figure the entire time.

"You cannot leave me here," Omar says, standing up.

"Actually, that's exactly what I am going to do," I say.

Omar looks up at me, panic in his eyes. "I'm sorry I killed your friend, alright? But I am desperate. Gamal's men will kill me if they discover I lost him this ring."

I walk over to Omar, the box pressing into my palm, and I stop when I am inches from his face.

"He wasn't my friend," I say, pushing my glasses up my nose with my free hand. "He was my family, you rat bastard."

I relax momentarily before I pull my fist back and

swing it, connecting to the left side of Omar's jaw, knocking him off of his feet and flat on his back where he remains, out cold.

I don't spare him another look. I turn around and walk into Griffin's outstretched arms.

Together we walk over to the ladder that will take us back up to the entrance tomb. The Professor climbs first, with me following behind him. When we reach the top the three of us lift the ladder out together and rest it on the ground.

"Should we push the stone back?" Griffin asks me.

"There's no need to bother," I shake my head. "No one will hear him yelling, and I'd like to disturb the area as little as possible. I'm sure there will be a team in here in a matter of hours after we notify the authorities."

"Still worried about the history," Griffin says, offering me a smile.

"Yes," I nod and my smile falters as I turn to look at the Professor.

He is standing over by Dr Cooke's body, his shoulders slumped forward as he stares down at his friend.

The tears lodge in my throat as I look at them.

"It wasn't your fault, June," Griffin says, reaching his hand out to me.

"Yes, it was," I whisper, not taking my eyes off Dr Cooke.

I turn and slowly walk over to the Professor, putting

my hand in his.

"He was my best friend," the Professor says in a low tone. "What am I going to do now?"

He looks at me, completely and utterly lost. I look back at him, mirroring his pain and all I can do is shake my head.

"We will take him with us," Griffin says, coming to stand beside me. "We can't leave him here. Not like this. Not with him."

Griffin looks over to the opening of the sunken chamber.

"I'll help you lift him," I say, and together we bend closer to Dr Cooke.

His mouth is slightly ajar and as I put my hand to his face his lips wobble slightly.

"Wait—did you see that?" I say to Griffin.

"What?" Griffin asks, kneeling beside me.

"He moved—his lips moved!" I say frantically, looking to Griffin.

The Professor kneels down on my other side and stares at Dr Cooke.

"Daniel!" he shouts.

Dr Cooke twitches at the sound and lets out a loud snore.

"He's—he's alive!" I yell, clasping my hand to my mouth.

"Daniel!" the Professor yells again, shaking Dr Cooke's

shoulder.

Dr Cooke's eyes snap open with a start and he looks around at us kneeling over him.

"What—what happened? What's going on?" Dr Cooke says, and makes to sit up, but groans and lies back down. "Oh yes, I've been shot."

"Been shot? You bloody died!" the Professor says, taking off his hat.

"I don't understand," I say, shaking my head. I reach down and pull up his shirt from his trousers. "It's just a flesh wound! It's only nicked your side."

I lift up his shirt higher for the others to see.

"But, why did he—" Griffin frowns.

I exhale and can't help but laugh.

"You passed out when you saw the blood!" I explain to Dr Cooke.

Dr Cooke's eyes widen.

"Blood?" he says, and I can see the colour drain from his face.

"Oh no, you don't!" I tell him sternly, putting down his shirt. "Just don't look down."

"A *flesh* wound?" the Professor looks flabbergasted.

"Help me up," Dr Cooke orders Griffin, who puts his arms under Dr Cooke and helps put him into a seated position.

"I—I can't believe it," I say, the joy bubbling through me.

"Are you sure that's all it is, June?" Dr Cooke shakes his head.

"You'll be fine," I say, putting my hand on his shoulder. "Disinfectant and a good bandage should do it."

"The first aid kit is in Clint's bag– Clint!" Dr Cooke gasps.

"I'll go and make sure he's alright," Griffin offers and quickly scrambles up and out of the chamber.

"What happened, June, did you find it?" Dr Cooke asks, grasping my hands and then looking down as he feels the box.

He looks up at me in astonishment and all I can do is smile.

"You found it," he breathes. "This is the discovery of a lifetime."

"No. This," I say, putting my hand to the side of his face, "is the best discovery we will ever make."

"A *flesh* wound?" the Professor repeats.

Griffin stumbles back into the chamber, supporting Clint who has his hand pressed against the side of his head.

"Clint, are you alright?" I ask, standing up to get a better look at him.

"I'm fine, just got knocked out," he says, shaking his head and wincing. "What did I miss?"

I open my mouth to answer but turn at Dr Cooke's voice.

"Well Albert, I would say we are finally even," Dr

Cooke says, picking up his hat off the ground and shaking it out before putting it back in place.

"Oh," the Professor purses his lips. "I'm not so sure about that."

"Not sure?" Dr Cooke says, and suddenly has enough energy to sit up straighter and turn to the Professor. "I took a bloody bullet for you, you ungrateful bastard!"

"Well, when you had died, perhaps," the Professor says, and reaches in his pocket to bring out his journal. "But now that it's a simple flesh wound."

"Simple flesh wound!" Dr Cooke blusters. "I saved your bloody life."

The Professor takes out his pen from his pocket and Dr Cooke tries to peer over the rim of the journal as the Professor starts scrawling.

"What are you writing?" Dr Cooke says trying to grab the Professor's journal. "June, what is he writing?"

I wrap my arm around Griffin's waist, and throw my head back in laughter.

Chapter Twenty-Three

"Right, I'm off," I say, shouting in the direction of the open door leading to the back garden.

When I don't get a response I walk through the kitchen, the counters laden with dirty pots and spoons. The bag of sugar is tipped on its side, half the bag's contents on the counter. I step around a glob of jam that's collected on the floor by the sink and walk out into the garden.

The Professor and Dr Cooke are seated on the wrought iron patio set, their hats on in the warm afternoon sun.

Dr Cooke leans forward to pour the tea into their cups while the Professor spreads a dark red jelly on his scone.

"I said, I'm off," I say, and they both look up at me. "Are you two stopping here?"

"We'll have to," the Professor says, returning his focus to the scone in front of him. "We've just made a new batch and it's finally set. We have to do a thorough tasting."

"Quality control is the most vital step in fruit preserves," Dr Cooke says, before taking a large bite of his own scone.

"Hmm… and I suppose tidying up isn't a high priority for you two?" I ask, raising my eyebrows.

"Creative processes can get a little messy, June Bug," the Professor says, swallowing his own bite of scone. "Can't rush perfection."

"Well I'd tidy it up before Mrs Stevens gets home," I warn. "She only just gave you your jelly privileges back."

"That woman is the queen of foreplay," the Professor chuckles. "It's all part of the chase."

I raise my eyebrows but decide to change the subject.

"I'm just off to the Ashmolean. The funeral cups of the Queen of Sheba are arriving today and I've been asked to have a look at them," I can't help the pride slipping through my voice.

Who would have thought that I, June Jenson, would be sought after to look at historical artefacts? It seems not so long ago that I was begging anyone who would listen to let me be in the same room as such significant pieces, but now I am asked to be the lead historian to examine them.

I've chosen not to renew my contract with Simon and the television network, even though the show had phenomenal ratings. They had a good go at convincing me otherwise, but after threatening to sue me and nearly getting us killed multiple times, I decided I'd had enough of television. To be honest, I wasn't the best at it. I might take a page out of Griffin's book and attempt a little writing of my own. In the meantime I've taken on a teaching position at a local sixth form college, in the hopes that I may be able to catch the students early enough and instill a bit of enthusiasm for history in them before they go off and conquer the world.

I heard from Carolyn, Thomas's wife, a few weeks after we returned. Apparently Thomas got cold feet at the last moment and they were able to make it to the British Embassy before Ahmed Gamal's men got a hold of them.

Again, she assured me of how very sorry he was for his behaviour.

I'm just grateful she called so she couldn't see me roll my eyes the entire time.

"The cups arrive today?" the Professor says, raising his hand to further shield the sun from his eyes while looking in my direction.

"Arrived this morning," I say to him.

I look at him for a moment and I see that same glimmer of intrigue in his eyes which has been a vital part of who he is for so long, but then I blink and it's gone.

"You go," the Professor says, turning his attention back to his tea. "You can tell us about it this evening."

"You're sure?" I ask, looking between the two of them, who are both now lathering another scone with a yellow marmalade. "I could use your assistance with some of the markings on the outer sections. I was looking through some of your journals last night, but I'm not entirely sure—"

The Professor raises his hand to halt me.

"Fear is a wonderful liar, June Bug," he says, and smiles. "Don't let it lead you down the rabbit hole. You don't need our help."

"More than capable," Dr Cooke mumbles through a mouthful of scone.

The corner of my mouth lifts.

"So you really *are* retired now?" I ask.

"You know how some people really look forward to something, but when it happens it's not quite as they imagined?" the Professor asks, taking a sip of his tea and leaning back in his chair with a sigh. "Well, retirement is *exactly* what I imagined it to be."

"Hear, hear," Dr Cooke says, raising his teacup to the Professor.

"Well you two make it look so easy," I say, offering a smile.

"Before you go, your lad has been looking for you," the Professor says. "I think he's at the end of the garden by the pond."

"Griffin?" I ask, a little puzzled. "What's he doing down there?"

"Albert and I went fishing this morning down there and we lost one of the poles to a rather nasty bass fish," Dr Cooke says. "He's gone in for it."

"In the pond?" I ask. "But it's ten feet deep."

"Had to get his swimming trunks on, didn't he?" the Professor shrugs. "It's a very valuable pole, June."

"I didn't even know we had bass in the pond," I say, looking into the far distance trying to see the pond between the grouping of trees at the end of the garden.

"Could have been a minnow," the Professor shrugs. "Bloody thing nearly took my arm off, didn't it Daniel?"

"Yes, well, I managed to pull you back, but I don't suppose I'll get any credit for that either, will I?" Dr Cooke says, crossing his arms across his chest. "I mean if taking a bloody bullet for someone doesn't get you the good fishing rod, I don't know what will."

I leave the two of them and make my way down to the end of the garden. I'm not sure what sort of mood Griffin will be in after he's had to swim in the mucky pond.

Swatting a fly as I wade through the trees I emerge on the other side to see the calm water, with no swimming Griffin in sight. Frowning, I turn to the right and then the left.

Suddenly I stop. Griffin is standing on the outer edge of the pond in the field that backs onto the green space where the wildflowers grow. I wave to him and he waves back but doesn't move.

I start to make my way over to him, my shoes sinking a little in the damp ground as I walk around the pond.

Finally, a few feet away from him I stop, and put my hands on my hips.

"The Professor says you were looking for me?" I ask, looking him up and down noting his trousers and sweater. "Did you get the fishing rod?"

"No," he says, and for some reason looks very nervous.

"Right, well don't bother," I say, shaking my head. "I'll just get him another one from the shops—he'll never know the difference. You'll never be able to see it in there anyways."

"June–" Griffin starts, and then suddenly stops.

"Yes?" I ask.

"I'm–" His eyes are wide and he lets out a shaky breath. "I'm a bit nervous."

"Oh there aren't any bass in there!" I say to him, laughing. "I just tell them that to keep them busy trying to catch one. I haven't stocked that pond in years. They've probably caught a piece of weed at the bottom."

"Not about the pond," Griffin says, wiping his palms down the side of his trousers. "About this."

I watch as he takes a deep breath and gets down in the midst of the flowers on one knee.

Oh God, what is happening?

"June Jenson, I know you said you didn't have to get married and you weren't even sure if you wanted to get married," Griffin says, his brown eyes not wavering from mine. "Well, I don't want to marry you."

I raise my eyebrows and am not entirely sure why, but a part of me wants to laugh at the statement.

"I don't want to marry you—I *have* to marry you," Griffin says, and takes a ring box out of his back pocket and opens it towards me. "And I hope you realise there is a difference."

I take a step forward and look at the red gemstone twinkling up at me from the gold setting.

"You're everything I've ever wanted, but never knew I needed," Griffin says, his brown floppy hair going wild in the breeze.

My hands shake as I continue to look down at his kneeling figure.

"Will you marry me?" he asks.

I study him for a moment before my face splits into a tremendous smile.

"Yes," I laugh, nodding my head.

Griffin lets out a huge sigh, his shoulders sagging in relief.

"Thank God," he says standing up.

He brings his lips down to mine, and in our little English garden, amidst the wildflowers, I fall in love with him all over again.

He pulls back, the boyish happiness etched on every line of his face. He places the ring on my finger before gathering me in his arms once more.

"Did you think I would have said no?" I ask him, laughing as I tilt my head back to look at him.

His face has a wide grin on it, the lines around his eyes crinkled.

"Those two spent the better part of the morning winding me up that you would say no," Griffin shakes his head. "They nearly ended up in the bloody lake themselves."

"Well?" I hear the Professor yell from behind me.

I turn my head to look over my shoulder and see the Professor and Dr Cooke coming through the trees at the edge of the garden.

"She said yes!" Griffin announces, and I can hear the pride in his voice. "I told you she would, didn't I?"

"Hmm," the Professor nods, and when he finally reaches us kisses my cheek. "Wonderful news."

"Congratulations, my dear," Dr Cooke beams beside him.

I hold my hand out to them, showing them the ring while the sun plays with the ruby.

"It was your grandmother's," the Professor says, looking at it fondly. "I hope you don't mind. I offered it to the young lad, when he asked for your hand."

"It's perfect," I say, looking down at the simple gold band with a claw setting.

"I was going to buy one, but when the Professor showed me this... well it just seemed so... *you*," Griffin offers.

I smile up at him, and nod.

"And with the savings, you'll be able to have a cracking honeymoon," Dr Cooke says, bouncing on his heels.

"Funny you should mention that, Daniel..." the Professor says.

I narrow my eyes at his forced casual tone.

"We just happened to come across a fascinating tour of the Samurai graveyard in Kotsuba," the Professor looks at Dr Cooke, who pulls a brochure out of his jacket pocket. "Their tombs are meant to be quite exquisite."

"You two are not coming on our honeymoon," I warn them.

Dr Cooke pauses momentarily, the brochure in hand.

"And I'm sure we don't want to go and see a bunch of Samurai tombs for our honeymoon," Griffin laughs, shaking his head.

"Oh, umm…" I purse my lips, turning my face to his.

"We… *do* want to see Samurai tombs?" Griffin asks, slightly confused.

"Well, I have heard very interesting things about the exhibit," I say. "I mean, we could just stop by on the way to a relaxing holiday, no?"

"Wonderful!" the Professor claps his hands together and turns to Dr Cooke. "I think the humidifier is still packed?"

"I'll check the coin collection," Dr Cooke nods, and they both turn and begin to walk back towards the house.

"You are not coming!" I yell at their retreating backs, but I can tell my words are falling on deaf ears.

I turn to look at Griffin.

"It will never be dull, will it?" he says, turning to look at me, smiling.

"Never," I say, taking his hand.

ABOUT THE AUTHOR

Emily Harper is the author of bestselling women's fiction novels White Lies, Checking Inn, My Sort-of, Kind-of Hero and the June Jenson series. My Sort-of, Kind-f Hero was the recipient of the RWA Reader's Choice Award.

She currently lives in Canada with her family.

Please enjoy a preview of Emily Harper's novel,

My Sort-of, Kind-of Hero

EMILY HARPER

Chapter One

She looked at the mass of rumpled sheets beside her and frowned; something was wrong. She tried to quiet her breathing, but the panic caused a pounding in her ears.

She expected this, so why was she so surprised?

Scrambling to stand up, she wrapped herself up in the thick duvet and ran into the main room of the cabin. The fire had died down but the remnants were still crackling in the hearth. She flushed with memories of the desire that had licked through her veins the night before in front of that very fire. Shaking her head in order to clear her mind, she looked to the door and saw that his boots were missing and his coat was gone.

Quickly, she ran to the door and flung it upon, unconcerned with the biting cold that snapped its teeth at her exposed flesh.

"So, when you invite someone to have coffee with you, do you normally sit there and write the whole time?"

I look up with wide eyes. To be honest, I forgot he was sitting there.

"I'll just be a minute, and you're early," I point out.

She couldn't stay out in the cold for very long, but needed at least another minute. He wouldn't leave like that; not without saying goodbye.

"Well, not to rush your artistic breakthrough here, but I

have to be back at work in fifteen minutes," Travis breaks into my thoughts again.

It's just so typical. I've had writer's block for days now—I literally couldn't write a coherent sentence—then about a minute before Travis walks through the door it's like the sea parted and Moses was on the other side looking relieved and waving at me.

It's pretty depressing when your mental metaphors are better than the crap you managed to put on paper that week.

They say when you have writer's block you should clear your mind and the 'inspiration' will just come. But my mind doesn't go blank, and I've spent the last three hours staring at the wall and wondering if you want French toast in France, do you ask for French toast, or just toast?

And now, because I've thought about it so much, I actually care what the answer is. Obviously not one of my better days.

And now Travis is here for our meeting, sitting across from me at the small bistro table, constantly checking his watch.

You know, I bet Julie Garwood doesn't have these problems. People understand that when her pen touches paper an invisible 'Do Not Disturb' sign is hung on her forehead.

The only thing on my forehead is bangs that were clearly a mistake.

Mainly because I thought I could cut them myself.

Travis is staring at me, idly bouncing his leg, and I'm torn between closing my notebook and being polite, or pretending I didn't hear him.

I've known Travis... well I can't remember a time I *didn't* know him, so we'll just call it a long time. He grew up in the subsidized apartment building a few blocks from our typical suburban house. He was a little... *rough*... growing up. My brother, Scott, brought him home one day, almost like you would a stray cat, and from that day forward it was like my mother had three children instead of two. Except Travis never lived with us; he went home every night to an apartment with a mother who just didn't care about her own son. I used to think that maybe if my parents hadn't looked after Travis growing up, his own mother would have stepped up, but I think they just saved him from the inevitable.

"You haven't even got a drink yet," I volunteer a solution. "And I wouldn't mind a refill."

His eyes take me in, probably assessing my stubbornness, which has always been a vital part of my personality, before he sighs and stands up.

Momentarily distracted from my creative breakthrough, I watch Travis as he goes to order his coffee; my writer's eye assesses him in an instant, turning him into a character from one of my books for a moment. It's a habit I don't ever seem to be able to turn off. It's actually a bit annoying really—especially when I've been trying to write my *actual* leading hero for the last few days, and all I've come up with is he has long hair.

Something tells me I'm going to need to give a few more details in the character description.

Travis is still wearing his winter hat but I can see the mop of black hair curling out from beneath it. His eyes are brown—just plain old brown. He's smiling at the barista, the dimple on the one side of his cheek ever present. He obviously has been spending time outside, as I can see the snowflakes have left their mark on his down filled vest, a flimsy plaid shirt underneath. Travis is the only person I know who wears only a vest in the middle of a Toronto winter. He always complains he is too hot. I don't leave the house without my fur lined boots and a Parka.

I would make him the best friend, I decide. I mean, I know that he's always been my brother's best friend, so I am slightly biased here, but he's just not how I picture my leading man. Though God knows enough girls seem to fall all over themselves to get to him. It's kind of tragic, really. And he has the physique for the 'leading man' for sure; his upper body is built from all his visits to the gym. But he's just too genuine. Not enough mystique there to be a smouldering hero.

Scanning the distant mountains her eyes freeze on the Northern hills. On the shadowed mountain range, way off in the distance, she could see the sight that her eyes had been searching for.

There, on top of the highest peak, he sat on his horse. The beautiful animal turned, its head pointing to the rising sun, supporting its rider. Although it seemed too far, she felt his penetrating gaze as it pierced right to her soul.

My pen stops and I bite the side of my cheek. And then what? She sees him, he sees her...

I look around and see Travis is still talking to the woman making his coffee. She's blushing and hanging on his every word. I could use this.

She's obviously goggling over him, prolonging the coffee making process so that he will keep talking to her. Everyone seems to be a sucker for that dimple. If he suddenly left and walked away, what would she feel? What would she do?

She'd probably wonder if she should keep making the coffee.

No—that's only because I've known him my whole life and don't get the fascination women have with him. To me, he's Travis, the boy who always pulls my hair and fidgets when I talk about sex.

But to this woman he could look like Mr. Darcy; he's got the hair for it.

From that giggle and blank look in her eyes, however, she's definitely not capable of pulling off Elizabeth Bennet.

Maybe Bella and Edward. She doesn't know anything about him and she's already smitten. Also, she keeps dropping everything. She'd be *perfect* as Bella.

She raised her hand, just to feel the connection, to feel that it was all real. But he was too far. The connection was slowly slipping out of her grasp - the wind carrying it to someplace beyond.

I puff out my cheeks and tap my pen to my lips. Think... Think...

Okay, he's on the hill. She can't get near him. He's leaving forever...

She watched as he reared his horse before turning and disappearing into the horizon. Lowering her hand she lifted her chin; watching, waiting, even though she knew the efforts were futile.

The table suddenly lurches from underneath me and my pen slides off the page. I look up to Travis, who has his hands raised in defence.

"Sorry, my foot kicked the table leg," he looks apologetic.

I look back down at my notebook and write the final words.

Into the howling wind she sighed and whispered the words that she hoped would find their way home. "Come back to me."

"Okay, let's do this thing," Travis says as I finally put down my pen.

"Okay, so I have all the food organized," I say, meeting his eyes again. "And you did the guest list, right?"

"Pretty much. I just did it on Facebook," he shrugs. "And your parents are okay with it being at their house?"

"I had to talk them into it, but I told them that thirty year olds don't make a mess like eighteen year olds do," I say, taking a sip of the drink Travis bought me.

He winces. "Yeah, I guess Scott and I got a little out of control that night. Man, it took us forever to save up the money to fix the broken windows."

I swallow my drink and frown at him. "Did you get me hot chocolate?"

"It's your favourite," he says, smiling.

"It was when I was five. Now I prefer coffee like the rest of the adult world."

"What happened to little Etty Lawrence? You remember: girl with the little blond curly pigtails, always trying to keep up with her big brother and his sexy best friend?"

"You're only three years older than me! You saw me go to prom, you saw me graduate university. And plus, it would be creepy for a thirty year old man to be taking a little girl out for drinks on a regular basis."

"You still order Shirley Temples, so I'm not sure you're helping your argument there."

Damn it, that's true. But I'm a sucker for those little swords with the cherries and orange slices.

"Scott doesn't suspect anything, right?" I ask.

"Are you kidding? He knows pretty much everything," Travis says as if there was ever a doubt.

"What? Did you tell him?" I accuse.

"Etty, he's turning thirty. He'd have to be a moron to not know there is going to be a party. You always order food from the same place, and we both live in a shoebox, so your parents' house is the only place that could fit more than five people. It didn't take Einstein."

I chew on my bottom lip.

"We will have to do something spontaneous," I say, nodding my head.

"Slow down," he says, holding up his hands. "Don't go crazy. The party we planned is fine."

Why does everyone always say that to me? Like they think I go overboard on everything.

Which is so untrue. Everything I plan is with love, and I am in complete control the whole time. It's the plans that have a mind of their own. I mean, did I ask the magician to put my mom in that box for his 'Disappearing Trick' even though my mother's claustrophobic? No. And after I calmed her down and she drank a bottle of wine I think even she appreciated that it was a pretty cool trick. And my dad fumbling with the keys to get her unlocked and punching out the magician—it was so romantic.

Sadly, I did lose my security deposit on that one.

"I know what you're thinking, but you don't need to do anything more than you've already planned. He's turning thirty, not going to space or something. Drinks, food and music is all anyone expects."

"Exactly, that's what they *expect*. We can't just have a boring old party or no one will remember it!" I argue. "How many times is my only brother going to turn thirty?"

"You used that argument to go to Montreal on your eighteenth. And when your dad turned fifty and we all went to Vegas. And when you hired reindeer for Lily's first Christmas. It's kind of been done now."

Honestly, a couple of reindeer get lost in the suburbs and you would think the world was coming to an end the way people freaked out. But my brother wasn't taking his daughter's first Christmas seriously. Is it too much for me to want her to have a firm grasp of Santa Claus? I don't want her turning out like Susan Walker from Miracle on 34th Street.

"Just leave it to me," I say, closing my notebook. "I have everything under control. He's going to have the best time ever."

"Should I have the fire department on standby?" he asks, smiling.

I offer him a fake laugh. "Ha, Ha. Very funny."

"So you have a signing tomorrow?" he asks, sipping his coffee.

"Yeah, not that there is much point. Two people at the last one. It was pathetic," I say, shaking my head.

I don't mention the two people were my parents.

"I'll try and stop by," he offers.

"You don't need to," I shrug. "I know it's not your kind of thing."

"If you're there, then it's my kind of thing. You know you're my favourite author," he says, offering me a lopsided grin that I know makes all the Bellas of the world swoon.

"I'm your only author," I counter. "You have one bookshelf which has like six books on it, and they're all mine."

"Seven after tomorrow," he winks. "I like to have a backup copy."

"I got another rejection yesterday," I say, sighing. "I'm up to one hundred and eight. Do you know what one hundred and eight rejections does to a person's self-esteem?"

"Maybe they don't know what they are talking about? Didn't that Harry Potter lady get rejected a bunch of times?" he offers.

"She got rejected twelve times. I still had hope after fifty," I argue. "They said they're looking for fresh, new ideas, yet every shelf of a bookstore nowadays has a sparkly vampire face staring back at you."

He nods in sympathy, though I can tell he has no idea what I'm talking about.

"I just don't get it. I get good reviews; everyone says my writing is great. I have the key components in my books: super-hot guy, strong woman. This next book even has a horse! Who doesn't love horses?"

"I don't really like horses," Travis says, but I shake my head at him.

"Maybe I just need to start fresh. A new angle. Completely change trains."

"What?"

I look at him frowning. "Change trains. It's a saying. You know, get off one train and go in the opposite direction for the next…"

His blank gaze makes me frown.

"Okay, just forget it. You know, you're not much help," I say, putting my notebook into my purse.

"They say you should write about things you know. You've never been near a horse," he says.

"I was at summer camp once. I broke my arm, remember?"

"Oh yeah, I forgot about that."

"Besides, I write historical romances. Unless you have a time travelling machine I don't know about, it's not like I can get any front line perspective."

"No travelling machine, unfortunately. Though you'd have to get in line for that one. First thing I would do is go back and warn my younger self to steer clear of Heather Morrison," he says and gives a fake shudder.

"Who knew the lawn of your apartment building could be that flammable? You should have just taken her to prom."

"She set the lawn on fire and we never even really went out. Could you imagine what she would do during a breakup?"

I laugh. "You have a point there. See, this is the problem. You have all these great stories, and I've got none. Maybe that's why my books suck. My imagination is letting me down."

"First of all, your books don't suck. They're good—I read one," he offers.

I raise my eyebrows in his direction. "Which one?"

"The one without a horse," he says, smiling. "And secondly, you have some good stories. Remember 'I love you Todd'?"

I can't help the blush of shame that comes to my face. "That's not worth repeating, let alone putting in print."

Travis is already laughing. This always happens. "It's the best story, though! He said 'I love you' to his dog and you thought he was talking to *you*."

I narrow my eyes as he tries to keep it together. I'm never telling him anything ever again.

"You're not helping my self-esteem right now," I argue.

"All I'm saying is people would probably like reading about *that* better than some girl mooning over a guy on a horse. Why don't you write about something that is popular right now? Figure out what people are into."

"Are you trying to say people aren't into historical romances?" I ask. "Because I'll have you know it is an extremely popular genre."

"I'm just suggesting that perhaps you should try to go for something new and exciting," he suggests. "Maybe write about something you know, something that has happened to you personally."

Alright, that is decent advice. Except the highlight of my love life has been Todd, and when you lose out to a Pomeranian it's not really something you want to share with the world.

"Listen, I've got to get back to work, but I'll see you tomorrow?" he asks.

"Hmm," I nod, non-committedly.

"Are you working at the comic book store this week?" he asks, tucking his chair under the table.

I work at the world's smallest comic book store in the Bloor West village. It's the only job that was even remotely close to a career in publishing, and they offer dental benefits. Well, kind of. The owner, Mr. Sharp, has a son who is a dentist, so I get a free toothbrush and toothpaste once a month. It sounds stupid but I look forward to that new toothbrush more than I should.

"All day, every day," I nod. "I have to pay for that shoe box apartment somehow."

"I'll stop by with a hot chocolate; I'm working just down the street from there," he says.

"Add a cookie to that order and I will consider opening the door," I smile.

"And don't go too crazy with the party, okay? Your mom will never forgive me if any of her new windows get broken."

Travis kisses the top of my head and makes his way out of the coffee shop.

Write what I know, eh?

Well, I *could* do a short story on magicians.